"Eavesdropping! How dared you stay around."

Tor tilted his head, his eyes dancing as if Emma's tirade were delighting him. "Beautiful," he exclaimed suddenly. "You look beautiful when you're riled."

Flustered, hating herself for blushing, Emma wondered what to say next. "Go, will you. Just go. Get out of here. Please."

"But of course," he said, stepping toward her. "All you had to do was ask."

She had stepped backward when he stepped forward, and her back was almost against the window. "Tor..."

"Take it easy. I'll see you... oh, just one more thing before I go." He glanced toward the telephone. "That man, Alan. You're not in love with him. No way are you in love with him."

Claudia Jameson lives in Berkshire, England, with her husband and family. She is an extremely popular author in both the Harlequin Presents and Harlequin Romance series. And no wonder! Her lively dialogue and ingenious plots—with the occasional dash of suspense—make her a favorite with romance readers everywhere.

Books by Claudia Jameson

HARLEQUIN ROMANCE

HARLEQUIN PRESENTS

Don't miss any of our special offers. Write to us at the following address for information on our newest releases.

Harlequin Reader Service
901 Fuhrmann Blvd., P.O. Box 1397, Buffalo, NY 14240
Canadian address: P.O. Box 603,
Fort Erie, Ont. L2A 5X3

A SECOND LOVING

Claudia Jameson

Harlequin Books

TORONTO • NEW YORK • LONDON
AMSTERDAM • PARIS • SYDNEY • HAMBURG
STOCKHOLM • ATHENS • TOKYO • MILAN

Original hardcover edition published in 1990
by Mills & Boon Limited

ISBN 0-373-03099-1

Harlequin Romance first edition January 1991

For Lars Thane,
my friend from the land of the midnight sun

CHAPTER ONE

'WHO was that, Sis?'

'I don't know, they hung up.' Emma Browning carefully replaced the telephone receiver and looked at it curiously. This was the second time today that somebody had hung up when she had answered the phone. She glanced at her brother through the archway separating his kitchen from his living-room, and decided not to make any comment about the calls. David was clearly in no mood for any kind of conversation, stretched out as he was on the settee, eyes closed, a frown creasing his forehead where it was visible under the mop of unruly blond hair which was so like her own. He looked so unwell, so tired, and, while Emma could barely remember the last time she had seen her brother suntanned, the pallor of his complexion now was alarming. But recovering from glandular fever was no fun for anyone, no fun at all.

She turned her attention back to the salad she was preparing and sighed inwardly, thinking how strange life was, how it could so easily and quickly make a mockery of the plans people made, if it so chose. Here she was, putting a light lunch together for her sick brother in his apartment in Newport News, Virginia, USA, on a gloriously sunny day at the beginning of June. It was not supposed to have been like this, though, for she had not been due to visit David until the middle of July. Not that it mattered particularly; her father was looking after her shop and it could not be in better hands. No, it was just that David was so poorly and ... well, her visit to America was supposed to have been a holiday and it was proving to be anything but.

A feeling of guilt washed over her and she turned again to look at her brother, chiding herself for the unworthy thoughts she was thinking. It wasn't as if David wanted her to stay indoors all the time; he kept telling her to go out, if only to take a swim. The pool belonging to the apartment building was tempting her yet again, and she could see it from the kitchen, but in the six days she had been here so far she had not even dipped a toe into it.

Nor, to be fair, had David asked her to come and look after him. On the contrary, he had tried to tell her over the telephone that he was fine really, just 'a little touch off-colour'. But Emma had known he was ill, she had just *known*, with the sort of knowing she had experienced many times in her twenty-four years. She and David were more than brother and sister, they were twins, born only fifteen minutes apart, and David should have known better than to attempt to deceive her because he, too, had the same sort of instinct when something was wrong in Emma's life, if instinct was what it was.

So she had made the transatlantic call to him just ten days earlier, late one night when a sudden feeling of uneasiness had kept her from sleeping, and she had finally got the truth from him, learning that he had seen a doctor that very day and that glandular fever had been diagnosed.

He had admitted to feeling ill for some time and it was typical of him to have walked around feeling ghastly for goodness knew how long, before giving in and seeing a doctor. That was one of the differences between them, one of the many differences. Twins they might be, bonded by love and understanding, in possession of this knowingness about one another, but they were as different as chalk and cheese in so many ways. For starters he was clever, extremely clever, and she was not. He was stubborn and she was not. She was artistic, creative, and he was not.

'David? You still awake? Lunch won't be long; would you like a cup of tea while you're waiting?'

'I'm not waiting.' The reply was mumbled, barely audible. 'I don't want any lunch, but the tea sounds like a good idea.'

Challenged, or at least feeling challenged, Emma turned again to look at him, deliberately keeping her voice crisp and firm. She was not going to let her brother's stubbornness work against him, not this time! Enough was enough. 'David, I have had quite enough of this nonsense. I've been here a week, and what you have eaten in the whole of that time would not make one decent meal for a normal man.'

'I'm not a normal man.' So his sense of humour had not deserted him, apparently. 'I never was.'

'I know that,' she agreed, stifling a smile, 'and your attempt to deflect me is not going to work. If you don't promise to eat this chicken salad, with at least two pieces of bread, I shall not make you another cup of tea for at least a week.'

David's eyes came open, brown eyes, soft and warm, like hers. 'Good grief, how long do you intend staying here?'

'Until you're better. Up and about. Recovered. But you won't recover if you don't eat.' She glared at him, her fingers crossed behind her back, hoping her threats were enough to get the man to *eat* something. Of course she could not stay here indefinitely . . . but David didn't have to know that.

'I wonder if it was Tor?' he said suddenly, his voice reflecting a surprising hint of anxiety.

'Tor? What do you mean?' Emma did not have to ask who Tor was because David had mentioned his name at least a dozen times since her arrival. He was David's neighbour, he lived in the apartment right next to this one and he was currently in New York visiting his father. There was little else she knew about this person except that he had obviously made a very favourable impression on her brother, which was unusual because David was not easily impressed by people. In fact, he was not a *people* person; David was a boffin, a scientist, and in her opinion he lived most of the time in cloud cuckoo land. His own private universe did not include matters of a practical nature—which was another of the differences between them.

'David?'

'On the phone. I wonder if it was Tor on the phone just now, ringing from New York?'

Emma shook her head. 'Of course not. Why would he hang up?'

There was a smile, the first he had managed today, but it was not news to her that most men made dreadful patients when they were ill; they always seemed to feel sorrier for themselves than women did. The smile was followed by a sigh. 'Because, Emma dear, my telephone was answered by a female.'

'So?'

'And today is Sunday.'

She was clearly missing something. 'David,' she said patiently, 'forgive me if I sound obtuse, but could you explain why my being female and today being Sunday might make your neighbour hang up when he telephones you?'

'He might have jumped to the wrong conclusion.'

'Ah!' A light was beginning to dawn. 'You mean he might have thought I was your girlfriend, that he was interrupting something?'

There was a satisfied nod, as if she had passed some sort of intelligence test. 'Yes. Except that I haven't got one.'

'Yes, yes, yes—but does *he* know that?' She was happy to prolong this silly conversation, if only to see more of the interest, the animation which had been missing in her brother all week. It might be a sign of recovery in him. 'Well, does he?'

'Yes.' The word came flatly, all animation gone now. 'It's probably the only thing we have in common—we're both off women.'

The temptation to point out that David had never been 'on' women, not to her knowledge at least, was one Emma resisted. Instead she asked why he got on so well with Tor if they had nothing else in common.

'It's just one of those things.' David's eyes had closed again. 'We just do.'

'And I can take it from all this that he didn't know I was coming here to look after you?'

'No. He'd left for New York before that was arranged.'

'I'll bet you haven't even told him you have a twin sister.'

'Of course I have. I happen to be very proud of you, you know.'

Emma hadn't known. She knew how much her brother loved her, but—David was proud of her? For what? Compared to his, her achievements were minimal. She was a florist running a modestly successful business, and he was employed, at a huge salary, by a vast chemical corporation whose network spread almost around the globe, an American company for which he had previously worked in England.

'Lunch,' she said pointedly, 'is about to be put on the table, David.'

Hours later she was saying the same thing about dinner, only to be disappointed again by David's lack of enthusiasm, his eating barely one quarter of it. She wondered whether loss of appetite always occurred with glandular fever, or was it just the way it was with him? What she did know was that time was the main healing agent with this enervating illness—and full recovery could take months.

'David, try, please. Finish the potatoes.'

'I can't.' He glowered at her, a warning not to nag, and promptly changed the subject. 'It's still hot out there—by English standards, anyway—so why don't you sit by the pool for a while? Or go to the movies or something.'

'I'm quite happy in the apartment, thanks.'

'Rubbish. You're bored. You just don't want to leave me.'

'Perhaps.' Emma smiled, but did not look at him. He knew, anyway. She was bored, and she wanted to see at least a little of America on this, her first visit to the country. All she had seen so far was the local shopping mall, though that in itself had been impressive. Everything was under one roof in one enormous building which was air-conditioned and spotlessly clean. There seemed to be no parking problems here, either, which came as an enormous relief. Driving on the wrong side of the road was nerve-racking enough, without having to negotiate David's over-large car—over-large compared to her own Metro—into difficult parking places.

Tomorrow she would have to shop again, just for food and a visit to the dry-cleaner, a pleasant prospect except for the driving. Well, maybe she would be used to driving on the right by the time she left. When would that be? A surreptitious look at David told her it would be a while yet, for there was no way she would go back to England before she had seen signs of *life* in the man.

England. Her thoughts turned to Alan, and she wondered how much he was missing her. He had only telephoned her once, to check that she had arrived safely, but transatlantic phone-calls were expensive. Still...they were engaged, had been since her twenty-fourth birthday at the beginning of March, and Alan Dobson was far from stingy when it came to spending money. Maybe he didn't like to make such long-distance calls on his parents' telephone? The fact that he still lived with his parents, at the age of twenty-five, never ceased to surprise Emma, who had long since left the nest and become independent.

She glanced at her watch. 'It'll be eleven-fifteen in England now, won't it? We are five hours behind?'

'Yes. Bit late to ring Mum and Dad.'

'I don't want to ring Mum and Dad, I want to ring my fiancé.'

'Go ahead.' David looked unimpressed. He had met Alan only once, the weekend before he'd left to live and work in Virginia, last January, and the two of them had seemed to get on well enough.

Emma got up, speaking over her shoulder as she headed for the telephone. 'I'll give him your regards, shall I?'

'By all means.' Then, shocking her, he added, 'He's a nice enough bloke, Emma, but I'll tell you this: Alan Dobson is not the man for you.'

'What? What did you say?' But she had heard, all right, it was just the way he had said it, with such certainty ... and it had come straight out of the blue! David had never made this comment before, nor anything like it, and it was more disturbing than Emma cared to admit. 'But—why do you say that? *Why*?'

'I don't know. It's nothing I can pinpoint. He just isn't right for you.'

'But——' She was stuttering, at a loss for words. 'You've only met him once. You don't begin to know him!'

'True. And I wonder how well *you* know him. You only met him at Christmas and you got engaged to him in March. A bit quick, if you ask me.'

'I didn't ask you, and that's a ridiculous thing to say, anyway. Three months is plenty of time in which to get to know someone.'

'A week is plenty of time to get to know someone.' David shifted himself lethargically from the table to the settee, where he stretched out and put his feet up, keeping one eye open to peer closely at his sister across the room. 'But there's knowing and knowing, it's a matter of degree.'

'And you don't know what you're talking about.' She had already started to dial, hoping to hide the disappointment she felt at David's disapproval . . . if disapproval it was. What he thought mattered to her, it mattered very much, but he really did not know what he was talking about. As the line clicked and the connection to England was being made, she repeated her retort with a hint of indignation this time.

'Don't get on your high horse, Sis. It's just—there was something about him that didn't jell with me, that's all.'

'Well, there's nothing that doesn't jell with me!' she snapped. But it wasn't true. Sometimes Alan was downright thoughtless, like the times he insisted they went out on the town when she was feeling tired after a busy day in the shop, on a Friday or Saturday. Or both. She couldn't fault him in any other way, though, and the allure of painting the town red would surely fade in its own good time, as he got a bit older and his interests and priorities changed. Once they were married he would have his new home, and her, and children to take up his time. Not that they had actually named the date, except that it would be in the spring of next year, eight or nine months from now.

Alan's mother answered the phone on its second ring, sounding sleepy. 'Marion? It's Emma. You're not in bed, are you?'

They were in bed. Worse, they had actually been asleep. Even worse, Alan's father had a summer cold and was feeling rotten. Worst of all, the call was in vain because Alan was spending the weekend in London. 'He's with Mike Nicholson, if you want to try him there, Emma.'

'No, I—it doesn't matter. Just give him my love.' With profuse apologies she hung up, noting that there had been no enquiry as to David's health but thinking nothing of it. After all, her future mother-in-law had not been fully awake.

'Is he out?' David wanted to know.

'Mmm.' Why did she feel disinclined to pursue the subject of Alan? 'I'll make some coffee.'

'Where is he? I mean, what is there to do at eleven-thirty on a Sunday night in Winchester?'

'He's in London, at Mike Nicholson's place for the weekend.'

'And who is Mike Nicholson when he's at home?'

'An old friend of Alan's, someone he went to school with.'

By the time the coffee was ready, David was asleep and the evening stretched out emptily before her. She could go to a movie, she supposed, but the idea didn't really hold any appeal. Besides, there was always something on the television here—and so many channels to choose from. She turned the set on quietly, but David woke anyway, just long enough to drink half a cup of coffee before going to bed. He couldn't seem to get enough sleep, yet he slept very lightly just now, which was most unusual for him. It had always been a joke in the family that David could sleep through an earthquake; as a boy and then as a teenager he had been almost impossible to wake in the mornings.

At ten that night the telephone rang again, and again the caller hung up without saying a word. No, it definitely was not Tor . . . Emma didn't know his surname, nor even his full forename. She replaced the receiver idly, wondering. What could Tor be an abbreviation of? Nothing sprang to mind, but then Americans did have a way of shortening names, of using diminutives quite different from English ones.

It was a left-hand turn that foxed her the following morning. Emma swung the car towards the huge car park at the shopping mall and clean forgot to stay on the right-hand side of the road. The result was a near disaster and she stood so violently on the brakes that David's car rocked in protest. She was bumper to bumper with a navy-blue Oldsmobile coupé and its driver was already leaping out, a look of angry disbelief on his face.

He didn't knock on Emma's window, nor did he signal for her to lower it, but simply flung the driver's door open and demanded to know whether she was 'off her trolley'.

She looked at him blankly. 'I beg your pardon?'

'I said, lady, have you lost your marbles? We drive on the right in this country.'

'I know, I . . .' In this country? Had he read her accent in the few words she'd spoken? 'I do apologise. I'm English, you see, and I——'

'And that's your excuse, I suppose?'

'No, I——' What? What else could she say, really? The near accident had not happened, and she had apologised. Perhaps she should do so again. Perhaps she would have, too, had he not been looking down his nose at her. His face was a handsome one, there was no denying that, but its blue, blue eyes were glacial, and there was a supercilious stamp all over its rugged features. From where Emma sat he looked intimidating, too, a good six feet tall and broad with it. Every contour of his muscular chest was visible through the white, skin-tight T-shirt he was wearing, and she really was not inclined to get into deeper argument with this man.

'I believe I've made my apology,' she said, with as much hauteur as she could muster, 'so, if you'll kindly close my door, I'll get my vehicle to the right side of the road.'

To her astonishment he started laughing, really laughing, while at the same time he bent suddenly and poked his head inside the car, right inside it. With a fearful lurch of her heart she flinched away from him, staring at his profile and his very blond, very thick hair. Neat hair, beautifully cut, not too long, not too short. 'What on earth do you think you're doing?' she demanded.

Demand or no demand, he did not answer her question. The full-bodied laughter had subsided to a rumbling chuckle and he was shaking his head now, straightening up again to look at her as if he had suddenly recognised her—which was of course impossible. 'But this isn't your car, is it? You don't look to me like the type who reads scientific journals.'

Emma's mouth opened and closed. From behind his car somebody tooted but she barely registered it, she was too concerned with the man's deductions, his correct deductions about the car, looking around as she was at the stack of David's journals on the back seat.

When she turned back again, the man had gone. He was in his own car and signalling for her to get out of the way. Determined not to get flustered again, she put the gear lever into reverse and drew back before driving forward and away from him.

'Arrogant creature!' She pulled to a halt in a parking slot and slammed the door as she got out of the car, muttering under her breath. But the incident was forgotten in no time, for it was far too beautiful a day to be spoiled by a stranger's bad manners. The sun was beating down from a clear blue sky and it felt good. Perhaps she would have a swim this afternoon—if David fell asleep. Maybe she could get him to go outdoors with her, to sleep on a lounger by the pool? She had not succeeded in that so far, but every day was a new one.

All she wanted from the shopping mall were a few special items from the deli that specialised in imported foods. If she could find some English marmalade, for instance, and the few other bits she had seen in here, little things she knew David liked especially, she might just stir his appetite into action. The rest of the food shopping would be done at the supermarket nearest the apartment block, near which was the dry-cleaner, and that would be it. The rest of the day would have to be filled with other things.

It was eleven-thirty when she got back to the apartment. 'David? You awake, love?'

'In here. Wide awake. I'm reading.'

Emma headed straight for the kitchen; she plonked the shopping bags on the counter and looked at her brother through the archway, thinking for the umpteenth time what a very lovely apartment this was. It had two bedrooms and was situated on the third floor of the building, overlooking a newly built marina and the James River. It was elegantly furnished in a style which suited

David not one iota, and the rent was being paid by his employers. Lucky David. If only he appreciated it. But an elegantly furnished apartment was not his style and it was very different from the flat he'd had on the outskirts of London. Different except for the books and the journals. They were everywhere, on his bed and under it, on his chairs and under them, stacked on the television, the coffee-tables, the floor. The bookcases were overflowing with them. Reading. It was all the man ever seemed to do outside of work. No wonder it made no difference to him where he was living. Provided he had his work and his books, he could be happy anywhere.

'I'm about to start lunch,' she told him, 'when I've had a cup of coffee. Want one?'

He did, and while they drank she told him of her close encounter in the car park, unashamedly, unselfconsciously, knowing she would not be laughed at.

'Takes some getting used to.' David nodded sympathetically. 'I made the same mistake three times during my first month here—it's easily done. Happily I never came bumper to bumper with anyone, though.'

'Well, I was just going into the car park, as I said. But he was a very arrogant specimen. Built like a Viking, he was, big and broad, blond and blue-eyed, very blue-eyed. Thick head of hair, quite gorgeous, actually. He was probably a Leo. David? David, what's the matter?'

She was being stared at. A slow smile spread across her brother's face before he spoke again. 'What sort of car was this person driving?'

'The Viking? An Oldsmobile.' It was the only American car Emma knew by make and model, simply because David drove the same vehicle. 'Exactly the same as yours, only in navy-blue.'

'I thought so.' The smile was almost ear-to-ear now. 'I just wish I had the energy to laugh,' he added, managing to do just that. 'Oh, how very apt your description!'

'What? What are you talking about? And what's so funny?'

'The Viking, as you call him. Why didn't I ever make that association? After all, he *is* Norwegian. Well, he's half Norwegian, his father is Norwegian but his paternal grandfather was Danish.'

'Who? Who are you talking about, David? You've lost me.'

'Tor. That was *Tor*, dear girl. Tor Pedersen, and he left here just fifteen minutes ago, just before you got back. But he didn't say a word about the incident in the car park! And, from what you've told me, he knew full well who you were. In any case, he must have known my car, let alone anything else.'

'Anything else? Like what?'

'Like you, you idiot. Could anyone miss the fact that we're brother and sister?'

'Hardly.'

'Well, then.'

Emma shrugged. 'So what of it?'

'So I'm wondering why he said nothing to me—but I'm no longer wondering why he looked amused when I asked him to come and have lunch with us.'

'You did what?'

'I said around one o'clock. I asked—you don't mind, surely? He's a super chap, Emma, he really is. I never dreamt——'

He never dreamt she would mind. In principle she didn't. It would be very unlike her to mind. She was a gregarious person, a people lover; she enjoyed dealing with the public and she had a wide circle of friends, so it would indeed be unlike her to mind having a guest to lunch.

'But you do mind, don't you, Emma?'

'No, not at all! I——'

'You mind. Why? Oh, come on, you're not going to hold it against him, are you? Give the bloke a chance, Sis. He only flew in from New York this morning and his first thought was to come and see how I am.'

'Correction. His first thought was to go to the shopping mall.'

'Mean. That was *mean*!'

Emma would hear none of it. A picture of Tor Pedersen flashed into her mind and she got meaner. 'OK then, maybe the big beefy hunk of rather-too-blatant masculinity fancies you.'

At that, David Browning laughed himself silly. His book slid from his lap and he rocked back and forth in his chair until tears streamed down his face. 'Oh, boy! Oh, Emma! You *can't* be serious? You can't really have thought him——'

Emma didn't really think anything of him. She excused herself and made for the kitchen, delighted to see her brother laughing like this. Laughter was a tonic, or so they said.

CHAPTER TWO

'TOR, I'd like to introduce you to my sister, Emma. Emma, this is Tor Pedersen, friend and neighbour.'

'How very formal, David. How very English of you.' The words came from Tor, but it was Emma he was looking at. 'But then the English are like that, aren't we?'

She blinked, nonplussed, and David was quick with an explanation. 'The other half of Tor is English, Emma, just to confuse matters further. The dear boy was educated at an English public school, just in case you were wondering about his accent and his occasional dig at English propriety—which he's more than capable of exercising himself.'

'I'm also capable of speaking for myself,' David was informed, but not unkindly.

'And if I might get a word in.' Emma held out a hand to the one being proffered to her, knowing she would get a warm-blooded, very firm handshake. She was right. 'I hadn't wondered about your accent, Tor. But now it's been mentioned, it does sound more English than American. It didn't earlier, though.'

A meaningful look passed between the men, and David grinned. 'Why didn't you mention the encounter in the car park?'

'And spoil all this fun? It had to be worth a laugh to you, David.'

Emma did not see what was coming next. It simply never occurred to her that David would do what he did, would actually *tell* his neighbour of their earlier dialogue.

Which was precisely what he did. No sooner had he lowered himself back into his chair than he came out with it. 'What gave me a better laugh was the conclusion Emma jumped to when I pointed out how thoughtful you'd been in coming to see how I was before you'd set foot in your own apartment today. She thinks you might fancy me.'

'David! David, I don't think that's funny.'

'Well, I do! Oh, Emma, you're blushing! Haven't seen you do that in years.'

She was blushing, too, furiously. And it didn't help that the object of this conversation was saying nothing, nothing at all. Tor's face was totally impassive, making his thoughts impossible even to guess at. He seemed neither amused nor annoyed—but what was he thinking?

After a moment, a very awkward one for Emma, he said, 'Is there anything I can do to help with lunch?'

'No. I—I mean, no, thank you. I—if you'll be content to talk to my wretch of a brother, I'll get on with things. I haven't much to do anyway.'

'And if I shan't?'

She stopped in her tracks, turning to face him, seeing at once the hint of amusement in his remarkable eyes. Just a hint, just a vague one, slight but unmistakable. 'Pardon?'

'What if I shan't be content to talk to your wretch of a brother? What if I'd rather come into the kitchen with you? What if it's David's sister I fancy?'

This had to stop. Right now. Before it got out of hand. 'Look, I'm sorry about that. It was said in a moment of—it was just a joke.'

David, who had been looking from one to the other and back again, quickly put his oar in. 'You have something against homosexuality, Sis?'

'Nothing whatever—as you know very well. Now stop it, David, because the joke has worn thin.'

'And you haven't answered my questions.' The Viking was watching her steadily, as if he was really interested in her response.

Emma turned and walked away, speaking at normal pitch from the furthest point of the kitchen, where the cooker was in the corner. 'If you have something to say to me, go ahead. As you can see, I'm not a mile away and I can hear very well from here. That's the one drawback with this apartment,' she went on, making a deliberate effort to be friendly with this man her brother thought highly of. 'The kitchen. I prefer a separate kitchen, with a door one can close—don't care at all for this open-plan idea.'

There was no reply. So much for her efforts at being chatty. With a mental shrug she got on with her cooking, wishing vaguely that Tor Pedersen were not here. His conversation with David was something she barely tuned in to while she moved around the kitchen, but she did hear a couple of comments. One was that his father never changed, and the other was that New York remained as frenetic as ever.

Lunch was not an easy time. David's neighbour seemed deliberately to stem her prolonged attempts at friendliness, answering her polite questions with minimal if not one-word answers.

'Do you work, Tor?'

'Now and then.'

'Doing what?'

'I write.'

Emma leaned forward with genuine enthusiasm at that. 'Really? What?'

'Oh, this and that.'

'Tor!' The protest came from David, who looked at the older man with a mixture of irritation and resignation. He turned to Emma. 'Tor writes all sorts of things, magazine articles, short stories—but he specialises in children's books and he's very successful. His pen name——'

The protest was from Tor this time, delivered quietly, as all his other conversation had been. It seemed that he was in fact a quiet man, when he was not shouting at someone who had almost crashed into his car. 'I don't think Emma expects a full history of my writing career.'

'Expects, no,' she said, smiling straight at him. 'But I've never met a writer before and I am interested. Bear in mind that your world is a million miles from the one I live in. All I really know about are flowers and plants.'

'But what she doesn't know about them,' David put in, 'isn't worth knowing.'

'I'm sure Emma doesn't need defending, either, David.'

There was a momentary silence, a look of puzzlement from the younger man. 'I wasn't defending what Emma does for a living, I was boasting about it.'

This was met with an oddly searching look, then 'Good. Well, that's all right then.' At which point the Viking turned to Emma and added, 'A world of flowers and plants sounds like a very beautiful one to me. I envy you that.'

Disquieted, she did not know how to answer him. She

had no idea whether he was being serious or whether he was patronising her. She simply could not weigh up this man, this person about whom she had had such a wrong impression just a few hours earlier in the day. 'I—what is your pen name? Might I have heard of you?'

'Possibly. It's——'

Again David interrupted. She wanted to kick him. Here, finally, she had dragged a bit of conversation from Tor—only to have it cut off by her brother. 'But I thought I'd told you this in one of my letters, Emma?'

She shot him a look of disdain. 'One of your letters? Brother dear, I have had two postcards from you in all the time you've lived here.'

'Oh. Well, didn't I mention it some time? I thought I had. Tor is otherwise known as Paul Fox. He wrote *Under the Honeysuckle*. Remember it?'

Remember it? She had loved that book as a child! She must have read it half a dozen times. It had been given to her on her eighth birthday and she still had it—somewhere in an old trunk in the attic. But how . . .? As the penny dropped, she stared at Tor and questioned him baldly. 'Good grief, how old are you?'

He smiled, his eyes lighting up wickedly. 'Thirty-four. Not as ancient as you might have thought.'

'He wrote *Under the Honeysuckle* when he was eighteen. It was his first children's book and it was a smash hit.'

'Thank you, David. What a good PR man you'd make.' But he did not, it seemed to Emma, appreciate David's extolling his virtues as a writer. David himself had said he had nothing in common with Tor—except that they were both off women, whatever that might mean—but they got on very well. She wondered again how this could be; the two were like chalk and cheese. For herself, she felt decidedly uncomfortable in his presence. He had a way of looking so directly into her eyes that she became insecure as to what he might be seeing there. What did he make of her?

She got up to clear the table at that point, deciding it really couldn't matter less what he made of her.

When she had stacked the dishwasher, she opted to make an escape. The opportunity of someone other than herself being with David was too good to miss in any case, quite apart from her wanting to be free of the discomfort she felt in Tor Pedersen's presence. 'Gentlemen, I'm going to leave you to chat,' she announced. 'I'll be down at the pool if you need me, David. It was nice to meet you, Tor. Well, it was for the second time!' she added with a smile she had to put effort into. 'I'll probably see you again some time before I leave.'

'Undoubtedly.'

Half an hour later, having given her lunch time to settle, Emma was swimming vigorously from one end of the pool to the other, stopping only when another length would have been a physical impossibility. As she started to haul herself up the steps, her eyes met with a pair of faded blue denims and travelled upwards to see a familiar white T-shirt. Her eyes narrowed against the glare of the sun right behind him, but the golden halo it cast around his hair did not go unappreciated.

'I—thought you'd be staying with David for a while.'

There was a grin, a flash of white teeth. Altogether a most attractive mouth. 'He fell asleep on me.'

'Don't take it personally, he does it all the time just

now.'

'Uh-huh. It'll pass, don't worry. It's all part of the recovery process.'

'I know, and I'm not worried.' She reached for a towel from the sun-lounger, grateful to be turning away from his gaze. Those all-seeing eyes had slid swiftly over every contour of her bikini-clad body and, while her figure was nothing to be ashamed of, his surveillance had quickly resurrected her discomfiture. When the excess moisture had been rubbed from her hair, she tied the towel around her waist and sat, dipping into her purse to retrieve her engagement ring and put it back in place. But throughout all this, she knew, Tor had been watching her minutely; she could feel his eyes on her.

'That's a beautiful diamond, Emma. I noticed it earlier, of course. Your fiancé must be a generous person.'

'Yes.'

He moved very lithely for such a well-built man, easily, assuredly, and without being invited he sat on the lounger next to hers. It was minutes before he spoke again, though; he seemed content just to stare across the James River, which was something Emma had spent many hours doing from David's third-floor apartment behind them.

The silence stretched on.

She wished he would go. They had nothing to say to one another and she was in danger of falling asleep herself. She lay back and closed her eyes, only to open them a moment later to see whether he was still there. He was, and she looked appreciatively at his profile, acknowledging privately how very handsome he was in a rugged sort of way. But why was he lingering here with her? Why didn't he just go about his business? When she could stand the silence no longer, she broke it.

'It's a gorgeous spot here. The apartments are very luxurious, aren't they? I suppose yours is a mirror of David's—except that it won't be as untidy. That would be impossible. But he's always been an untidy so-and-so, he used to drive Mum mad when he lived at home. Basically, David is a very shy man, you know.'

'What?'

It was obvious he hadn't heard a word. It was almost laughable, the way he turned and looked at her blankly. Not one word had registered with him! 'I—was just saying that my brother is basically very shy.'

'I know that.' He turned away again. Another conversation stopper. Two full minutes passed before he spoke again—leaving her conscious of another silence. 'I'm an observer of people, Emma, it's part of my work. I knew that about David within two minutes of meeting him.'

'But you're not shy. A man of few words, perhaps, but you're not shy. I—well, I'm intrigued to know how you and David get on so well.'

When he turned around this time, Tor's eyes fixed deliberately on to hers and stayed there. 'That's simple enough. David and I can enjoy a silence. Unlike you, he doesn't feel the need to rush in and fill one. You should try sharing a silence some time.'

A feeling of irritation ran through her. She knew what it was to share a silence with someone—but she couldn't with him. Not only was he a stranger, but he was a disconcerting stranger at that. 'I think I'll go indoors now. I don't want to have too much sun in one go.' She was already gathering her things together, pushing her feet into her sandals.

'Will you come out to dinner with me tonight?'

Stupidly, her mouth fell open. This was the last thing she'd expected and she was stuck for words. There were so many reasons why she would not dream of having dinner with this man, she hardly knew where to begin her answer.

'A simple yes or no will do, Emma.' He squinted up at her, eyes narrowed against the afternoon sunlight.

'No.' It came out ungraciously and she heard it, adding hastily, 'But thank you for asking.'

'I'd like to reciprocate for the splendid lunch you gave me.'

'Well, there's no need. Bye. See you around.'

'Wait.'

She stopped, stilled by something, some indefinable thing in his voice, in that single word. 'Yes?'

'Never let it be said that I can't take no for an answer. I can. But would you mind telling me, just for my own entertainment, why you're declining my invitation?'

'By all means. Firstly, I wouldn't dream of leaving David alone all evening. Secondly, I happen to be engaged, and I don't think Alan Dobson would relish the idea of my having dinner with another man.'

'And thirdly?'

'There is no thirdly,' she lied. She lied and he smiled; fully and knowingly he smiled, but he didn't push the point.

Instead he said simply, 'David does not need a babysitter.'

'I disagree. In any case, there are still the feelings of

my fiancé to consider.'

'Can I take it he calls you here every night?'

'I—no, but that's beside the point.'

'I see.' He stood, dwarfing her five-feet-seven in sandals, inclining his head with an elegance that belied everything about his physical build. 'So be it. Then, as you say, Emma, I'll see you around.'

She felt slightly unhinged when she got back inside the apartment, unhinged and more disturbed than any of her three encounters with Tor could possibly call for. What was it about him? What a curious mixture of a man, this Anglo-Norwegian whose home was America, this watcher of people who volunteered very little about himself. Tor Pedersen, alias Paul Fox, author of a book she had so loved and cherished, written by him when he was so young. It was all a little difficult to assimilate, really, but one thing was for certain: if she lived next door to him for the next three years, she could never get to know him. Not that she wanted to. There were far too many contradictions about him, complexities she would not even want to begin to unravel.

So, when the doorbell rang at eight-thirty that evening, Emma braced herself for a fourth encounter, not dreaming it would be someone other than Tor. As she swung the door open in response to the bell, however, it was to find there was nobody on the doorstep. She was staring at nothing when David's voice reached her from the living-room.

'Wrong bell, idiot. That's the second time you've got it wrong. Pick up the phone to your right and press the button. Someone's calling from downstairs.'

'Don't you call me an idiot! I'm not so security-minded

myself. Hello? Who? Just a moment, please. . .' She traipsed back to the living-room, not wishing to call to David from the hall. If this were an unwanted visitor, for it was certainly an unexpected one, then she would have to use a little tact and get some guidance from David. 'Hey, you with the book, there's a female by the name of Anna O'Brien come a-calling. Are you home? I mean, are you home and, if so, are you available?'

He gaped at her, seeming stunned. 'I—I—*Anna*?'

'That's very unhelpful, David.' Emma was grinning, intrigued, and about to say what Tor had said to her earlier: 'A simple yes or no will do.'

'I—well, yes. I mean yes, and yes, I'm available! But I wonder why . . . I mean I wonder what . . .?'

His sister left him to his wondering and told Anna O'Brien to come right up. She waited in the doorway to greet this mysterious visitor. David had certainly been flabbergasted—but was she right in thinking he seemed tickled pink?

One look at Anna O'Brien, Miss Anna O'Brien, gave Emma her answer. Any man would be tickled pink by a visit from this lovely creature. Long jet-black hair demurely tied back at the nape, an impossibly flawless, peaches and cream complexion, eyes nearly as black as her hair, almond-shaped, lashes longer than any Emma had ever seen—this was Anna O'Brien.

And she was blushing, too, making her look even lovelier somehow. 'I . . . please forgive my intrusion. I—you must be David's sister. I'm—well—we work together. I mean, not in the same laboratory but—er—for the same company. I—David and I are . . . that is, we talk together in the dining-room . . . sometimes.'

Preventing laughter required self-control on Emma's part. This girl was nothing less than enchanting, and if Emma felt like that about her what did David feel? They talked together in the company's dining-room 'sometimes'? And what else? What was this supposed to mean?

'How very nice to meet you, Anna. Yes, I am David's sister. I'm Emma. Do come in. David is up, if not exactly up and about!'

'He's no better, then?' The black eyes looked anxious. 'Perhaps I shouldn't have ... I didn't know you were here, you see, until today. Somebody at work mentioned that they'd called David and ... shall I come back some other time?'

But they had already reached the living-room and to Emma's amusement she saw that David had not only cleared several stacks of books from chairs, he was also blushing as furiously as Anna was!

So what should she, Emma, do with herself? Leave them alone or what? 'I was just about to brew some fresh coffee, Anna, would you like a cup?'

'Yes, please.' Her shyness was excruciating, making David seem almost voluble by comparison. From the kitchen Emma watched and listened, without appearing to do so, unable to help herself.

'How are you feeling, David?'

'Not too bad, thanks. Can't come back to work yet, though. Doctor's orders.'

'I—hope you don't mind my calling?'

'I'm very pleased to see you, Anna. I always enjoy our chats at work. I think it's kind of you to come and see how I am. I ... didn't realise you knew my address, actually.'

Emma turned her back squarely to the archway at that point, chiding herself and her desire to laugh. It was just so . . . so *sweet*. There they were, obviously quite enamoured of one another, not knowing what to say next. What a dope David was! Had he never asked Anna out, for heaven's sake? No, of course he hadn't. And there was no question as to the identity of yesterday's silent telephone caller now, either. What agony she must have been through, wanting to know how David was feeling but not daring to speak to a female voice. What had she felt when she had learned, today, that David's twin sister was over from England?

Relief, as a close approximation!

Half an hour later, after gauging the situation, Emma said something about thinking about taking a stroll, getting a bit of fresh air.

'It's a bit late to go out on your own now, Sis. I mean, you don't know the neighbourhood and . . .' He rattled on a bit but he needn't have bothered. Emma got the message. His eyes were imploring her not to leave him alone with Anna. Poor darling, did he think he'd never be able to handle this situation without the comforting presence of his sister? What on earth was he afraid of?

'Perhaps you're right.' She paused, looking from one to the other. Anna's eyes told her nothing; they were fixed on the carpet. 'I'll finish my letter to Mum and Dad instead.'

'What letter?'

'The one I started when I went to bed last night. I'm giving them a detailed report on you.' Impishly she winked at him, glancing quickly at the top of Anna's head. 'I'll join you a little later.'

Half an hour should do it. If she left them to their own devices for half an hour, they should be able to break the ice fully.

Unfortunately it didn't work out like that. Twenty minutes later there was a knock on her bedroom door and Anna poked her head around it. Emma looked up quickly, surprised. 'Don't tell me he's fallen asleep on you?'

'No, no, I . . . but I should be going now. It's, well, I don't want to tire him. He doesn't look very well, Emma. Nice to meet you, anyway.'

'I hope to see you again,' Emma put in quickly, feeling both for her and for David. Was this a case of like attracts like? So shy, the pair of them! 'Maybe you'd like to have dinner with us later in the week, Anna? How about Wednesday? You could come straight from work.'

'Oh, I'd love to!' There was no hesitation, only pleasure. 'But shouldn't we check this with David?'

'No need. He's not going anywhere and it's obvious to me that he likes your company.'

'Do you really think so?'

Emma cleared her throat, allowing only a small smile. 'That's certainly my impression, yes. So we'll see you on Wednesday; I shall expect you when you arrive. Is there anything you hate to eat?'

'Kidneys and cabbage.'

'Right. Well, I think we can all live a day without either of those. I'll see you out.'

'I'll see her out.' Suddenly David was there, almost protective of Anna, glancing with open suspicion in Emma's direction. 'What have you been telling her about me?'

'Not a word, David. Not one single word.'

He asked the question again as soon as Anna had gone. 'I said nothing about you, I just invited her to dine with us, that's all.'

'You what? When? Why?'

Emma looked heavenward. 'I invited her to dinner. On Wednesday. As to the why of it, I knew it would please you. Go on, deny it if you dare!'

He responded with a defiant shrug. 'I'll have you know that Anna is a very bright girl, very bright indeed. She's *Dr* O'Brien; she has a PhD in——'

'Never mind her qualifications, David. More accurately, you might say she's ravishing.'

With a sheepish grin, he conceded, 'She is rather pretty, I must admit.'

'Rather pretty? She's beautiful!'

'She's also two years older than me. Do you think that matters?'

'To whom? It obviously doesn't matter to her. She likes you very much.'

'Do you really think so?'

Emma's eyes moved heavenward again. 'I despair of you. How can you be so clever in some respects and so very dim in others?'

'Thanks.'

'No, the age difference matters not in the least. And yes, I really do think she likes you. She came here to see you, didn't she?'

'All the same, I'm not sure about Wednesday. What will we talk about all evening?'

'What do you talk to her about in the dining-room at work?'

'Our work.'

'I'm sorry I asked. What do you know about her? I take it she's an American?'

'Third generation, Irish descent. Parents both dead. She shares a house with two others girls, in Smithfield. That's across the river.'

'Is that it?'

'That's about it, yes.'

'Well, on Wednesday you'll learn more about her.'

He brightened suddenly, swinging his legs down from the arm of the settee as if he'd just had a new rush of energy. 'I'll ask Tor to join us, that'll ease the situation.'

'No! Oh, no, David. Definitely *not*. I'll keep things flowing if you're seriously in danger of drying up, though I think you do yourself a discredit. Just relax and be yourself, the way you are with me—and with Tor. You had no trouble getting to know him, so let it be the same with Anna.'

'Don't be silly. It's different with Tor, he's very, very easy to talk to and—well, he's male.'

'There's no arguing with the second part of your statement.'

'You didn't like him.'

'I didn't dislike him.'

'Emma. . .'

'It's true. I don't know anything about him. Well, hardly anything. Which reminds me, why on earth hadn't you told me he's Paul Fox the writer? You hadn't even told me he was a writer, let alone the author of half a dozen brilliant children's books!'

'I thought I'd mentioned it.'

'The trouble with you, David, is that you spend half of your time with your head in the clouds. If it isn't stuck in a book, it's definitely not down on earth with the rest of us.'

'You'd never guess to look at him, would you?'

After a heartfelt sigh, Emma answered that with an expansive shrug. 'Now what are you talking about?'

'Tor. You'd never guess, to look at him, that he writes those beautiful, sensitive stories.'

'In a word, no. Never.'

'I think he's a dark horse.'

'That makes two of you, after what happened here tonight.'

'No, seriously, he's a private person. I'm the only one in this apartment block who knows he's Paul Fox.' This was added with almost childlike pride, a very endearing way David had about him at times. 'He's not a bit egotistical, you know. He doesn't go around telling people who he is.'

'Then he obviously trusts you, it's a compliment.' Emma looked at her watch; there had been no telephone call from Alan and it was too late to ring him now. It was three in the morning in England. Why hadn't he phoned? Marion would have told him about her trying to reach him last night. It was odd. If only she'd thought to ring him earlier, but there had been distractions. 'I'm going to bed, David. See you in the morning.'

'At ten o'clock? That's not like you.'

'Yes, well, one way and another it's been an unusually full day for me. Happy reading.'

'I'll be off myself shortly. Goodnight, love. And, Emma . . . thanks for everything.'

She blew him a kiss and scarpered. The rest of her letter to her parents would wait till tomorrow. They would ring here before they received it anyway.

By eight the following morning the letter was finished. For the past half-hour Emma had been sitting in glorious morning sunshine, dressed only in shorts and a matching top in canary yellow, feeling bright and well rested and generally at peace with the world. Her early night had enabled her to wake early, too, and she had taken advantage of the fact that David was still sleeping to come outside at seven-thirty to enjoy the sort of heat England rarely enjoyed even at the height of summer. Here they would have months more of it because it was only June and, from what David had told her, from what he had been told by the locals, it could stay like this until the end of September. There would be storms, though, inevitably, according to the locals, but she wouldn't mind that in the least, she found storms exciting and had never been afraid of them.

She heard the sound of the shower running when she went indoors. David was up; she would make breakfast. Ham and eggs, *Virginia* ham and eggs, of course; maybe the smell of them cooking would stir his appetite . . .

'Now what was that?' She spoke to herself aloud, wondering whether she had just heard the outside bell or the internal buzzer. Or was it the other way around? 'Oh! So it was the bell. I'm—oh, never mind. Good morning, Tor.'

'Good morning.'

Was he looking at her expectantly? What did he want at eight-thirty in the morning? 'David's in the shower.'

'May I come in?'

So that was why he was looking expectant, he wasn't used to being kept on the doorstep. 'Of course.'

'Something smells good.' He followed her towards the kitchen, hard on her heels and speculating. 'Bacon?'

'Ham.' And she was not, not going to ask whether he would like some. 'As I said, David's in the shower.'

'Yes. I did hear you, Emma.' He looked down at her, seeming amused for some reason. 'Surprisingly, that colour suits you.'

'Why surprisingly?'

'Yellow looks awful on me, and you're nearly as blonde as I am.'

'I'm not nearly as blonde as you, nowhere near it.'

'Maybe it's the difference in the eye colour. I thought the combination of brown eyes and blond hair unusual when I met David but it looks even more unusual on you. Maybe because you're rather lovelier than he is.'

'Not true.' She turned away to tend to the ham. 'David is lovely in his own way, I'm just the feminine version, that's all.'

There was a bark of laughter. 'I can't figure whether that was a modest or immodest remark!'

'I shouldn't try. Why are you sounding more American this morning?'

'Much depends on my mood.'

'I see. I think.' It was hard to resist a smile. 'Er—did you want something, Tor?'

'Why, Emma! Haven't you guessed? I came personally to accept your invitation to dinner tomorrow night.'

She groaned inwardly, knowing her face must be giving her away, knowing and not caring. 'I'm—glad you can make it.'

He was laughing, at her rather than with her, because

she wasn't even amused. 'You knew nothing about it, did you? I thought not, I guessed as much when David called me last night.'

'He called you? When you live right next door?'

'Conserving his energy, no doubt. Anyhow, he asked if I would help him out of an awkward spot tomorrow night but he didn't explain what he meant. He said that that would keep till today. He said also that you very much wanted me to come.'

'Oh, he did, did he?'

'Uh-huh. Lying in his teeth, of course.'

Emma looked away, unsure how to respond. The heck with it, why should she protect David? 'Yes, he was.'

'I wonder why?'

She told him why, she told him about Anna O'Brien's visit, about David's unmistakable interest in her and his anxiety to have other people around in case he got tongue-tied with her. She was staggered to learn that Tor already knew about her.

'David mentioned her to me about a month ago. He asked her out to a party but she said she couldn't make it. He never asked her again, however,' he added, grinning, 'because he didn't have the nerve. That's what he said. I told him he was crazy, that everything indicated Anna's being genuine when she said she couldn't manage the party—but it made no difference. He said he'd lost courage.'

'It doesn't surprise me in the least. I'm—I wonder why he hadn't mentioned her to me?'

'You're put out, aren't you? Because he mentioned Anna to me but not to you.'

'Yes.'

'Would you mind not talking about me as if I were not here?' David was standing in the doorway of his bedroom, watching them. He wasn't dressed, he was wearing only his towelling bathrobe and he looked rough. Tor said as much.

'I feel rough,' David admitted. 'If you're cooking that food for me, Emma, stop right there. There's no way I could handle ham and eggs, or whatever you're planning to give me. Sorry, love, but I'm going back to bed. It's pathetic, I *feel* pathetic. Honestly, all I did was take a shower—and I feel shattered, as if I've used up all my juice.'

'I'll bring you a cup of tea in bed.' Emma was already reaching for the kettle.

'No. Thanks all the same.'

'Coffee, then.'

'No. Honestly, Sis, I don't want anything.'

'But, David——' She was moving towards him as he retreated into his bedroom, but she didn't get very far. A large, strong, restraining hand was on her shoulder and she glared up at its owner furiously. 'Don't interfere, Tor! Let go of me.'

'You're fussing. Flapping. Like a mother hen. It's ridiculous. Just let him be.'

She attempted in vain to push the hand away. 'Let go of me. I want to see he's all——'

'He is all right. I went through the same thing myself when I was around his age. All he needs is to rest, so let him. Just let the man *be*, Emma.'

Her response was an odd mixture of emotion, part relief, part resentment, part disbelief. 'You've had glandular fever? But what business is it of yours, anyway? Move out of my way while I——'

Tor didn't move out of her way, but moved instead to block her path entirely, his free hand catching hold of her chin, forcing her to meet his eyes. Heavens, such incredibly blue eyes! 'Emma, you are not your brother's keeper.'

'The same could be said of you. David doesn't need you to protect him, most especially from me!'

'Maybe he does. Your staying indoors all the time is bugging him, he told me so yesterday. He's starting to feel guilty because you won't go out.'

Emma, for her part, was so conscious of his hands on her, on her face and on her bare shoulder, that the irony of the situation nearly escaped her. 'But—this is so silly! I'm more than happy to be here with him and——'

'No, you're not. You wanted to see something of America, at least of Virginia. Come for a drive with me. I'll take you to Williamsburg, you'll enjoy that.'

'It's out of the question,' she said flatly. 'You saw how he looks. He's feeling terrible.'

'He's feeling tired, that's all, it's not the same thing. He'll probably sleep all morning. And what of you? More knitting?' He glanced towards the knitting she had left on a coffee-table yesterday. 'Or television, perhaps?'

'For the last time, Tor, let go of me, please!'

He let go of her. 'The phone's ringing.'

'I'm neither as deaf nor as daft as you seem to think me,' she snapped, reaching for the wall-mounted phone in the kitchen. '*I* know what's best for my brother!'

'What is best for your brother?' It was Alan, which she regretted in the circumstances. 'Who are you talking to about David?'

'I'm—just a neighbour.'

'But what's going on?'

'Nothing, Alan. He was just leaving.'

'He?'

'Yes, David's neighbour. Oh, never mind, Alan. Tell me how you are.'

Damn Tor Pedersen! He was leaning negligently against the huge refrigerator—from what she had seen on TV, every American home had a huge refrigerator; she had yet to see a small one in an advertisement or a film. She waved a hand at him, signalling that he should leave now, that this was private, but the wretched man just stood there.

'Has he gone?' Alan wanted to know.

'Y-yes, he's just left.' She was blushing to the roots of her hair, hating her observer and his insolence. She made a fist at him but it provoked only a smile. 'What did you say, Alan? What do you mean, checking up on you? Of course not. It wasn't midnight, it was eleven-fifteen. I didn't know your parents would be asleep, they don't normally go to bed . . . well, how could I know your father had a bad cold? The answer to that is simple, I didn't get around to ringing earlier, that's all. I assumed you'd be in the pub and . . . no, I was not checking up on you! When did I ever do that?'

She had turned her back on her observer long before Alan came back with, 'OK, OK. So how's David?'

'Not good.'

'Does this mean you won't be back for a while?'

'Not for a couple of weeks, I should think.' He didn't sound disappointed, exactly. Or did he? It was hard to tell. 'Alan? It's just . . . I want to see some real sign of life in him before I leave. Why?' She put a smile in her voice, forgetting, fleetingly, that she had company. 'Are you missing me? That's good to hear . . .'

Behind her, Tor quietly cleared his throat and she spun round to glare at him. She would not put it past him to make a background noise that would have Alan asking questions again. 'Look, Alan, I'm just in the middle of cooking breakfast, actually, and since you're calling from the office, perhaps . . . yes, darling. OK. Yes, I'll talk to you soon. Bye. Take care.'

Tor spoke first, beating her to it, the moment the receiver connected with its cradle. 'So you did call him darling, finally.'

'What? Now, look——'

'I take it that was Alan the fiancé?'

'Of course it was Alan, my fiancé. What——'

'The man you intend to marry?'

Frustration made her voice rise. 'What else does one do with one's fiancé? Of *course* I intend to marry him, that's why I got engaged to him!'

'I wonder——'

'*Don't* wonder!' She almost shouted the words. 'Just go, will you? How dared you stay around like that? Eavesdropping. I can't believe it, I just can't believe the audacity of it!'

He tilted his head to one side, his eyes dancing as if her tirade were serving only to delight him. 'Beautiful!' he exclaimed suddenly. 'As they say in the movies, you look beautiful when you're riled.'

Flustered, hating herself for blushing at a remark which was not only trite but also insincere, Emma put her hands to her temple and wondered what to say next. 'Go, will you? Just go. Get *out* of here. Please!'

'But of course,' he said, stepping towards her. 'All you had to do was ask. Politely.'

She had stepped back when he had stepped forward but there wasn't much further she could go. Her back was almost against the window. 'Tor. . .'

'Take it easy.' He got as far as the cooker and switched the frying-pan off. 'Your ham's burning. I'll see you . . . oh, just one more thing before I go . . .'

'What? For heaven's sake, what?'

He glanced towards the phone on the wall. 'That man, Alan. You're not in love with him. No way are you in love with him.'

CHAPTER THREE

EMMA was not one to bear a grudge, she never had been. Squabbles, fights, rows, she had always been able to put things like that into perspective, at least after a night's sleep, and generally to forgive and forget. So she could forgive Tor Pedersen and his unmitigated gall in saying what he had said, in doing what he had done yesterday morning. . . but she was not about to forget it in a hurry.

Five o'clock, Wednesday afternoon, found her standing in her room before the full-length mirror in the wardrobe—or rather the closet, as it was known in America—surveying her appearance critically. She wanted to look her best because she felt she needed every ounce of composure, of confidence, to face yet another encounter with her neighbour. Thank heaven he was only her neighbour temporarily!

She had dressed in pink, which was definitely her colour, the one which suited her best of all, in a very fine cotton shirtwaister with a full skirt. White high-heeled sandals together with white, good-looking costume jewellery, just earrings and a simple 1920s-type string around her neck, added nicely to the effect. Wearing her hair up added the touch of sophistication she wanted. It was piled high on her crown but the curls of her deep fringe added some softness. She would do. A quick spray of *L'Air du Temps* and she was ready.

Anna arrived first, but only just. Tor came within two minutes of her being seated comfortably in the living-room, just as if he had listened from next door for her arrival. Maybe he had. Anyway, his timing was perfect. Introductions were made and Emma saw with a mixture of gratitude and resentment that Anna seemed pleased by the presence of a fourth person. How cosy! she thought cynically. A foursome!

From the kitchen she looked at David and found him watching Anna's exchange with Tor. Somehow, the Viking was managing to put the girl at her ease in record time; Anna was laughing delightedly and David could not take his eyes from her. It didn't bother Emma, though; not for one moment did she think that Anna's interest might switch from David to the brute, the undeniably attractive brute, from next door. Anna was interested in, if not already half in love with, David Browning, whatever the man was or was not.

'Tor?' At an appropriate moment Emma stuck her head through the archway and gave him a facsimile of a smile. The one he gave her in return was equally false.

'Emma?'

'Perhaps you'd like to see to the drinks? I'm sure you know where everything is.'

'He does, but I'll get the drinks.' David was already on his feet. . . how different from the David of yesterday morning! 'What would you like, Anna?'

'I. . . don't drink alcohol, David.'

'Not at all?'

'Not at all.' Her eyes shifted to the carpet briefly before meeting once more with his, looking for disapproval or approval, for a reaction at least.

'How odd!' David was almost staring at her. 'Because I don't, either, and I've always thought people would consider me stuffy. . .'

'I don't think it's stuffy. I mean, I wouldn't think you stuffy. . .'

In spite of herself, in spite of everything, Emma found her eyes shifting towards those of Tor and, this time, the smile they exchanged was a real one. It spoke, as they both silently acknowledged, of their appreciation of what they were witnessing. David and Anna, both perfectly grown up and capable, both highly educated and in love with their work, behaving just as cats behave when they first leap on to the lap of a stranger: testing the ground, feeling around, seeking safety before, finally, hopefully, settling down to purr contentedly.

By the time eight o'clock rolled around the conversation was flowing and the dinner had been pronounced a success. Emma had taken pains over it because David had been so concerned about doing things the American way, which meant serving a salad before, not with, the main course. For dessert she had done one she did especially well, Baked Alaska, which also had been a success. She and Tor between them had gone through a bottle of wine, plus another quarter of a bottle, and when she'd suggested it was time for coffee he had insisted on making it and serving it.

She let him; she also let him stack the dishwasher and was quite content to do so. He seemed very familiar with the apartment and where things lived in it, which prompted her to wonder how many meals the two men had shared since David had moved in here last January. In six months or less they had become firm friends, enough, probably, to have shared meals in one apartment or another. She wondered idly what Tor's apartment was like. Was it also rented or did he own it? How was it furnished? Like this one or quite differently?

'Emma?'

'Mmm?' To her chagrin she realised she had been on the verge of falling asleep. Goodness, how rude of her! And she didn't have the excuse of its being stuffy in the apartment, for the air-conditioning prevented that. It had to be, simply, the meal and the wine that had made her sleepy. 'Sorry, Tor, what did you say?'

'I was suggesting we take a walk. You look as if you could use some air and I would appreciate some company.'

She didn't even think about her reaction. As she met the Viking's eyes, they shifted fleetingly towards the other two and she got the message at once. 'I'd love that. Anna? David?'

They didn't hear. They were engrossed in conversation which was over Emma's head. Science. More specifically, chemistry. More than that she could not define.

'David, Tor and I. . . Anna? Sorry to interrupt, but Tor and I are going to take a walk.'

'Oh. Yes. Fine.' Had she really heard?

'It's a beautiful night,' David added, a bit lamely.

'Do you want to join us?' This came from Tor, who knew very well what the answer would be. The question made Emma bite her cheeks.

'Er—no, not this time. I'm—Anna and I are going to have another cup of coffee before she goes.'

Tor and Emma departed at that point. Rapidly. Silently. Leaving the others to enjoy one another alone. It had been a very successful evening, as Tor remarked as soon as they had got out of the building. Prior to that, nothing was said. Nothing was said after it, either.

Under the light of the moon, he offered Emma his arm and she linked her hand through it as if it were the most natural thing in the world, as if she had been doing it for years. 'A successful evening, Emma. Mission accomplished, I'd say.'

'Agreed. Well done.'

'Well done, you, too.'

She did not notice how much time slipped by as they walked, as she looked at apartment buildings and up at the night sky, as clear as crystal and star-studded. She watched passing traffic, not knowing they could have taken a very different, far more private walk than this. They could have been by the river, they could have sat under the scarlet awning at the back of their apartment building, where one could sit where the white tables and chairs were, watching the traffic at a distance, a mere trickle at this hour, driving across the bridge over the James River. There they could have sat in the night air, speculating, perhaps, on the other inhabitants of the apartment building, on their lives and their reasons for choosing to live there. All sorts of things.

But they walked in a main thoroughfare instead. In silence. And Emma did not notice that a full hour slipped by. Her hand remained tucked under Tor's arm and while she was far from being unaware of his presence, she was unaware of the absence of conversation.

'Emma?'

'Mmm?'

'It's midnight. Perhaps we should go back.'

'*Midnight*?' It jolted her so much that she pulled her hand away from his arm with unnecessary speed, as if he had just said something deeply offensive to her. 'Midnight?' she repeated herself, to cover her sudden embarrassment at her odd behaviour. 'I'm—yes, we should go back, we should go back.'

Tor said nothing for a while. Disconnected, they walked; they walked until they were almost back at their building and it was only then that he spoke again. 'I enjoyed this evening, thank you.'

'You were——' She had to say it, it was only fair. His presence had been very helpful earlier. Credit where credit was due. 'You were super with Anna. You were a help.' She paused, wondering if it would seem outlandish, wondering if she should say what was on the tip of her tongue. It had just come to her, this knowing, from nowhere. 'Tor, do you know something? About Anna and David, I mean. My brother——'

'Your brother is going to marry that girl.'

'Good heavens!' It stopped her in her tracks. He turned, smiling, a questioning look in his eye, and all at once she was talking with the rapidity of a machine-gun in full flourish. 'That's what I was going to tell you, that's just what I was about to say! But how did you know? How could you know? You're right, you are absolutely right. David doesn't know it yet, of course he doesn't know it yet, but he *is* going to marry Anna O'Brien.'

Tor didn't comment, he was still smiling, just smiling. His hand reached for hers, only to find that her hand had moved half-way to meet his. Then their hands linked, fingers intertwining automatically, involuntarily, but for Emma there was the sudden consciousness of a touch against her engagement ring and it was another jolt, something which stopped her in her tracks not literally this time but mentally.

What was she doing?

Here she was, engaged to be married, taking a moonlit stroll with a near-stranger who had begun, against her wishes, to intrigue her a little too much. How had this come about? What had happened to her irritation with him?

The answers were not difficult: she was out walking with Tor simply to give David the opportunity of being alone with Anna. As for her irritation, it had, again quite simply, just dissipated. So what was she fretting about? It wasn't as if she were doing something wrong.

Nevertheless she eased her hand from his and, for the want of something better to say, she asked him how long he had lived in his apartment here.

'You don't have to make conversation, Emma.'

'I know I don't. I'm just interested.'

'I doubt it. That wasn't a spontaneous question, it was contrived because you grew uncomfortable holding hands with me and you want to put me at a distance again, and not just physically.'

Her eyes closed briefly. He was too perceptive, far too perceptive for her comfort. 'That isn't true,' she lied. 'I was merely wondering how long you've lived in this part of Virginia.'

'OK. Almost two and a half years. I moved into the apartment six months after my wife died.'

'*Died*?' Emma stopped walking again, was staring up at him in shock. 'But—oh, I'm so sorry, Tor! I had no idea. I just assumed. . .'

'What? That I was the perennial bachelor type?'

'No. Actually, no. I assumed you were divorced.'

'Really? Why is that?'

'I'm not sure. Just a remark David made. He said the only thing you and he have in common is that you're both off women and so. . .' She had begun to feel foolish.

'Well, that clearly isn't true in David's case. No more than it's true of me,' he added, his eyes steady on hers. She saw the pain in them, the pain that this mention of his dead wife had provoked. 'The first two years were the most difficult time of my entire life,' he went on. 'Painful doesn't begin to describe it. Suffice it to say I never want to go through something like that again. . . but I'm a healthy, normal, red-blooded male and about six months ago I started to come to life again.'

Meaning what? That there was a woman in his life? Emma found herself hoping this was the case. She decided to ask him outright. 'So there is someone now? A woman?'

'No one woman, no. I'm not looking for that, for that sort of relationship.' He paused, started walking again and added, 'I'm not looking for a permanent relationship of any kind.'

Anna had left by the time they got back and David was still awake, awake and animated. He thanked Tor profusely for being there that evening and tried to insist he came in for a nightcap.

'No, David. Thanks, all the same. I'm going to work.'

'You're going to work? Now? At this hour?' It was Emma who expressed surprise. David, apparently, knew his neighbour kept peculiar hours. 'Do you often start work at this time of night?'

'When the mood takes me. One can't write to order, Emma. Or I can't, at any rate. When it's ready to come, I let it come. It's a wonderful catharsis, you know.'

She could understand that readily enough, but what was it he wanted to get out of his system just now? What was it that had put him in the mood to write in the wee small hours? And what would the subject be? Something for adults this time? Something about the pain he had experienced on losing his young wife, perhaps?

'Did you know he's a widower?' Emma asked this of her brother the moment Tor had left. 'That his wife died almost three years ago?'

No was the answer to that. David looked thunderstruck. 'Grief, no! I assumed he was divorced.'

'So did I.'

'A *widower*? He's never mentioned that, never mentioned a wife at all.'

'Then it's my turn to feel complimented,' she said. 'I suppose. Anyway, so much for Tor. What about Anna?'

'She's marvellous! Don't you think so, Sis?'

'Marvellous,' Emma smiled. 'But that wasn't quite what I meant, dear heart. Did you ask her out? I mean, will you see her socially once you're feeling well enough to go out?'

'Certainly.' Such confidence, all of a sudden! 'And in the meantime, she's coming here again. On Saturday, for starters. She's going to spend the day with me.'

With me. Not with us but with 'me'. So where did that leave Emma? It was not yet time to return to England but ... but she wouldn't be needed on Saturday, not with Anna here to cater for David's needs.

'If only I could shake off this lassitude,' he was saying. 'I'd love to take her out for the day, to wine her and dine her, so to speak.'

'You will, love, just give it time. As for Saturday—er, would you like me to absent myself?'

'No! Absolutely not. Anna's taken a liking to you.'

'That,' she said, 'is as maybe. But you're lying in your teeth, David. Oh, well, we'll just let Saturday sort itself out, I can always spend the day by the pool. Come to think of it, I'd enjoy that enormously.'

Saturday did not sort itself out, Saturday was sorted out for Emma by Tor. When she came in from the supermarket on Friday afternoon, it was to find him and David deep in conversation.

They were sitting opposite one another, David on the settee and Tor sprawled in an armchair, his long legs stretched out. The sight of him came as a shock to Emma. She had seen nothing of him since Wednesday night, had heard not one sound from his apartment and suddenly here he was, big and broad, his very presence dominating the atmosphere. She wanted to stare at him, to study in detail his barely clad body. He was wearing only a pair of denim shorts, ragged at the ends, as if they had been cut off from a pair of jeans. Flung half over his shoulder, half over the back of his chair, was a beach towel.

That chest! It was magnificent, matted with hair several shades darker than the blond of his head, just as his legs were, exuding strength, power. The entire package exuded power.

'Hi, Emma. Our neighbour has emerged, as you can see. He's been in hermit mode since Wednesday night, just stopped scribbling an hour ago.'

'Hello, Tor. What are you two so deeply in conversation about?'

'Politics.'

'Bor—ing!'

'I agree. But your brother wanted to know more about the way the US of A is run.'

'Ah. American politics. I'm sure they're just as boring as English ones.'

There was an appreciative smile, a full and slow surveillance from those incredibly blue eyes. 'You're looking very cool and crisp. Pale blue suits you almost as much as that pale pink you were wearing the other night.'

So he had noticed. She had assumed her efforts at looking very presentable had been wasted on Wednesday. 'I'm not cool and crisp,' she said bluntly. 'I'm hot and bothered. I'm going to unpack these groceries and go for a dip in that delicious-looking pool out there. I take it that's what you've just been doing, Tor?'

'Nope. I'm on my way. I'll join you, if you don't mind.'

And what if she did? She could hardly prevent him from swimming! 'Sounds good. Why don't you come out with us, David? You could sit on one of the loungers.'

'Emma, you've been saying that to me every day since you arrived. I do not want to sit in eighty-five degrees' worth of sunshine watching other people have fun in the swimming pool.'

'Fine. Then sit in the shade and read a book.'

'No.'

'Just for the sake of getting some fresh air.'

'*No*, Emma!'

She looked at Tor, 'As you see, my brother can be very stubborn at times.'

'Like his twin,' came the quiet reply.

The water felt marvellous. Emma swam the first length gently before challenging the Viking to a race of six lengths.

'Six?' He threw back his head and roared with laughter. 'You haven't got a hope!'

'What do you mean? You're not telling me you can't manage six lengths, for goodness' sake?'

'In this little pool? Know something? You're a very sweet girl, Emma Browning.'

'But you're not going to take up my challenge, right?'

'Wrong. It's no challenge, it's no contest. Why don't we make it interesting, let's make it twenty lengths.'

'Done.' She did not expect to win, not over that distance, but she certainly didn't expect him to leave her standing the way he did, either. She had thought herself a strong and fast swimmer, but she had to think again. Tor cut through the water with all the grace and speed of a panther and when finally she pulled herself out of the water to sit, breathless, next to him on the side of the pool, all she could do was laugh. At herself.

'I think you made your point.'

'Come on, now, no sour grapes.' Suddenly his arm was around her shoulder and she drew away, hating the way she liked the feel of it there.

'I—think I'll stretch out for a while.'

They both stretched out, side by side on loungers. Five minutes later, Tor announced that he was taking her out for the day tomorrow.

'No, you're not.' She opened her eyes to look at him, only to find that his eyes were on her, more specifically on the curve of her breasts. Mortified, she glanced down to discover that one breast was almost totally exposed. She rapidly adjusted the bra of her bikini and raged inwardly at her negligence. The thing was too skimpy altogether, she had worried about it when she had bought it.

Very quietly he said, 'No arguments this time, Emma. You're spending the day with me tomorrow, and that is that.' She was just about to argue in earnest when he added, disconcerting her utterly, 'And, by the way, you're blushing again. It's very sweet but it's quite unnecessary, you know. I have seen breasts before, even completely naked ones.'

'Tor——' She did not want to hear this sort of talk. Coming from him it was disturbing.

'It'll be a mystery tour,' he said, lying back again and closing his eyes.

'It won't be a mystery tour.' The temptation just to look at him, to feast her eyes on him while his own eyes were closed, was more than she could resist. 'It won't be anything because I'm not going out with you.'

'You're doing it for David.'

'To hell with that. In any case, I'm planning to spend the day out here, right here in this very spot.'

Tor didn't answer that, he merely spoke her name, very softly, very quietly. 'Emma.'

'What?'

'You've forgotten to put your engagement ring on again.'

She thought about that when she was in bed that night. It didn't mean anything, not a thing. She had merely forgotten to put her ring back in place after emerging from the pool. So what?

And what if she had agreed, finally, to go out with Tor tomorrow? That didn't mean anything, either. Between him and David she had been put on the spot; not to accept Tor's offer would have been churlish if not downright childish. It was no secret that she wanted to see something of Virginia before she went home. It was no secret that she would have been doing just that with David had she come here as planned next month. David had a two-week vacation during July and. . . but things had changed, changed drastically.

How little she knew of Tor. There were so many questions she had wanted, several times, to ask him, but David's remark about his being a very private person inhibited her. He knew next to nothing about her, either, come to think of it. Perhaps he had no further curiosity about her. Or maybe he thought the details of her life would be boring. Maybe they were.

Alan had rung tonight, around six-thirty, but she had been in the shower and David had answered the call. 'No message in particular,' Alan had said. 'Just let Emma know I'm at Mike Nicholson's for the weekend, if she wants to reach me here.' There had followed Mike's telephone number, which she already had a note of anyway. Eleven-thirty, English time. Another weekend in London with Mike. Doing what? The discos and clubs and pubs, of course. That was very much Alan's scene and there was plenty to choose from in London. He loved London, had suggested that they live there once they were married. Emma wasn't keen on the idea. Oh, she liked London well enough but not to live there. In her eyes, Winchester left nothing to be desired and the capital was in easy reach from there anyway.

And with whom?

Was it likely that two good-looking, twenty-five-year-old bachelors would spend their evenings on the town without any female company? Not if Mike Nicholson had anything to do with it. Alan could be trusted, though, she was more or less sure of that. Never once had he given any sign of taking his engagement to her lightly.

But did she care that much? What if Alan were to make a transgression, would it be the end of the world? The end of their engagement? No, it would not. She would hardly be able to blame Alan, given the circumstances. In the six months she had known him they had had three arguments, three serious arguments, and they had all been about sex. The last one had been five weeks ago and it had been pretty violent, in fact it could have been the end of their engagement, simply because Alan had made the mistake of giving Emma an ultimatum.

'So what are you telling me?' she had shouted. 'What exactly are you telling me, Alan? That if *I* won't sleep with you, if I won't go *all* the way with you, you're going to take someone else to bed? Or that we're finished? Or both?'

'Yes.' He had been shouting, too. 'No. I mean, no, of course not.'

'That's about as clear as mud. Yes, then no? To which questions, Alan?'

'Look, Emma, I don't *want* someone else.'

'But there are no guarantees, right? Well, go ahead! I'd only have myself to blame, wouldn't I?'

'Emma, Emma, I wasn't threatening you, I love you. For heaven's sake, listen to me, please. . .'

She had listened and, within ten minutes, they had made up and put their argument behind them.

Her mental meanderings were halted by the sudden awareness of music emanating from the next apartment. Tor's apartment. It was very faint, a little melancholic. What was it? Mozart? Beethoven? What was he doing?

She looked at her bedside clock. One-ten a.m. She had been in bed for almost two hours and had not yet slept a wink.

Thinking? Writing? Remembering, perhaps.

Whatever, it was no concern of hers, was it?

CHAPTER FOUR

'YOU and David have an older sister, haven't you, Emma?'

'Yes. Janice. She's almost thirty and heavily pregnant with her third baby. No,' she amended, smiling, 'her third and fourth babies, she's expecting twins. We don't see much of her because she lives in Devon and leads a busy life. Mum and Dad see more of her; their being retired gives them the time. But I work six days a week in the shop, so it isn't easy to get away.'

Emma leaned back in her seat and cast her eyes over the menu she had just been given. She had enjoyed a marvellous feeling of freedom all morning, being well away from the confines of the apartment, and Tor was proving to be a wonderful companion. He had collected her early and had driven straight to Richmond, saying that the capital of Virginia was the first thing she should see.

Well, she had managed to see quite a lot of it, on foot and by car, and she'd been snap-happy with her camera, using an entire film before they had stopped to rest and have lunch.

'I'm starving.' She smiled at Tor over the top of the menu, her dark brown eyes lit with pleasure and anticipation. 'But I'm *not* going to stuff myself too much.'

'Why not?' He was smiling, too, looking at her as if she were all the entertainment he needed today. He had told her twice already how much he was enjoying himself with her, enjoying her enjoyment, as he'd put it. 'Why hold back if you're so hungry?'

'Because we're going to be walking around Williamsburg this afternoon—and if I eat too much, all I'll want to do is sleep.'

'You can sleep in the car on the way there.'

She gave him an admonitory look. 'Don't encourage me, Tor!'

He leaned forward, closing the small space separating them across their table for two. His eyes were amused and gentle on her face, a faithful reflection of what she heard in his voice. 'You're far from self-indulgent, I think you need encouragement. My impression is that you're altogether too strict with yourself.'

'Is it? And what would you know?'

'I don't know. As I said, it's my impression.'

Her smile was non-committal as he went on, 'Tell me more, Emma, tell me about your life, your lifestyle.'

She decided to have the chef's salad. 'Not much to tell. I left school at seventeen knowing exactly what I wanted to do. I'd known that for years. Since I was very young, I'd helped my father in the shop whenever I had the chance, after school and at weekends. Until I was twelve, we'd lived in the flat, it's a big one on two storeys, above the shop, so I was brought up with flowers around me. My mother never had any interest in floristry, nor did my siblings, but I learned everything my father could possibly teach me. He's a marvellous florist, you know, and happily I inherited his flair, his artistry. I worked for him full-time when I left school and he took me buying with him in the early mornings——'

She broke off when the waiter reappeared to take their

order, reassuring Tor that the chef's salad would be enough to keep her going for the afternoon. The restaurant was almost full and she looked around at the very varied clientèle, quite forgetting what she'd been talking about until Tor prompted her.

'Go on.'

'Mmm? Oh. There isn't much more. When I was twenty-one my father decided to retire early. He was fifty-seven by then and he said he wanted to enjoy himself with Mum while he was still young enough to. They take frequent holidays these days. And good luck to them, I say.' The smile her last words provoked was almost off-putting because Tor seemed to be smiling against his will. 'What's so amusing?'

'Nothing, really. It's just that you have a delightful way of adding bits of information with—it doesn't matter, Emma. Go on.'

She hesitated, wondering whether the last part of her story was too private to be divulged, and deciding that was silly. 'Well, it had always been understood that I'd take over Dad's shop one day, so when I was twenty-one he sold the business and the premises to me. He sold it to me at less than its value and, in order to be fair about things, he gave David and Janice a lump sum of money each. He was happy to do that: he said we all might as well have part of our inheritance now, while he was still around to see us enjoy it. He's always been clever with money, and he has all sorts of pensions and endowment schemes tied up. Had there been any problem about my getting a loan to buy the premises, Dad would have given me a private mortgage. But there was no problem, I'm glad to say. I wanted Dad to have the capital, as he would have had if he'd sold it to somebody else. And that's about it, Tor, the story of my life. I pay my payments to the bank each month and I manage to make a decent living—and I'm very happy with my work.'

'Hardly the story of your life,' he put in. 'What were you like as a child? What did you do during the years you lived over the shop? I mean, before you were old enough to start working, or rather creating, with flowers?'

Creating with flowers. It was a nice phrase; it pleased her because it was in fact accurate. Feeling thoroughly at ease with him, she answered his questions, talking about herself and her formative years until their food arrived.

The chef's salad was enormous. She should have known; helpings in America were generous to say the least.

'And you still enjoy painting?'

'Very much.' She eyed the food with a frown between her brows. 'And reading, and knitting and crocheting.'

'Don't you go out much? Your life sounds——'

'Dull?' she interrupted. 'I have made it sound that way, haven't I? But it isn't. I do go out——'

'Hang on, there. Don't put words in my mouth. I said nothing about dullness. I was thinking only that your work seems to predominate. Is your work so important to you?'

'Important, yes, in that I enjoy it very much. *So* important. . . that depends on what you mean. I don't live to work. It isn't the beginning and end of my existence. I have no qualms now, for example, about being away from my shop for several weeks. Mind you, it helps knowing that it couldn't be in better hands. I dragged Dad out of retirement for a bit!'

'And what of the future?' he persisted. 'What of Alan? What does he do, what does he want for his future?'

Emma glanced down at her plate and started eating, keeping her answers minimal now. 'Alan sells computers. He's quite ambitious and he wants what I want—our own house, a nice lifestyle, holidays, nights out, two or three children.'

'Nights out and two or three children?'

Her voice was a touch defensive, as she heard and privately told herself off for it. 'We can have both. We can have it all if we can afford help around the house, possibly someone living in.'

There was a silence. It went on for so long that Emma was forced to look at him, wondering what he was thinking, but the blue eyes were telling her nothing. There was no amusement in them, there was only their steady probing as he looked into her own eyes. With a self-conscious flush she glanced away, determined to change the subject. 'How's your steak?'

'Wonderful! Marvellous!' Emma looked at Tor with a broad grin, appreciative of his patience. He had, of course, seen in the past everything there was to see in Williamsburg, but for her it was a totally new experience and she was loving it. It was unlike any other place she had seen, a living museum immaculately restored and preserved to show its millions of annual visitors what life was like in Colonial times.

'Marvellous for the prosperous,' she went on, 'but imagine being a slave in those times.'

'I'd rather not.' He took her hand and linked it under his arm as they stepped outside into the glorious sunshine on Duke of Gloucester Street, the wide, tree-lined street that was the main thoroughfare through Williamsburg.

There was so much to take in, the horse-drawn carriages, the people strolling around in clothing as it had looked some two hundred years ago, the beautiful houses and gardens. The gardens! So colourful and profuse with dogwood, lilies, peonies, hollyhocks, roses, periwinkles—a feast for the eyes, most especially those of a florist.

'What were you saying earlier, Tor, that Williamsburg was named in honour of King William the Third?'

'Mmm. He ruled the Colonies at the time it was born.' Smiling down at her, he added, 'That was, of course, before the resentment of British rule began to grow.'

'A resentment that resulted in the War for Independence.'

'Right. Let's take a swift look at the apothecary shop before we visit the Wythe house.'

'What's the Wythe house?'

'One of the most beautiful here. George Wythe, one of Williamsburg's most accomplished men, was, among many other things, the first Virginian to sign the Declaration of Independence.'

'But—how come you know all this?'

There was a shrug, a casual smile. 'I'm a mine of useless information.'

'Rubbish! Either you have a very retentive memory and you can recall things you learned years ago in school—or you've taken the trouble to read up on this place. Now, which is it?'

'The latter,' he admitted, seeming delighted by her perspicacity. 'And only recently at that.'

Emma laughed, tucking her hand more snugly under

his arm as they walked into the eighteenth-century drugstore, listening with interest as Tor went on.

'I like to learn about the area I'm living in, no matter where that might be, no matter how young its history—comparatively speaking,' he said.

'Compared to England's, you mean?'

'Or Norway's. Whatever. Now then, cast your eyes over these elixirs and ointments and whatnot, then we'll get the "apothecary" over there to show you the leeches they used for bleeding people.'

'No, thank you!' He might have been teasing her, but she was taking no chances on it. '*That* I can live without!'

'Chicken!'

'Yes, I am, I am.' She held up both hands, laughing and enjoying herself more than she had in a very long time. The authenticity of the apothecary shop, including all its alien aromas, was as fascinating as the old milliner's they had just spent time in. Too much time, probably, because it was impossible to see all there was to see here in half a day.

It was turned six o'clock by the time they got back to Newport News. Next on their agenda was a swim; it had been agreed hours earlier that they would swim before changing to go out to dinner.

'And where are we going to eat tonight?' Emma asked the question when they stretched out on loungers after a particularly non-energetic time in the pool. She was wearing a stark white swimming costume rather than the too-revealing bikini she had worn the other day. She opened her eyes, reminded by the memory of her embarrassing moment that she had not put her engagement ring back on. She could feel Tor watching her as she dipped in her bag for it, though he made no comment other than to answer her question.

'There's a severe shortage in this area of the type of restaurant I'd like to take you to. If we were in London or New York it would be a different story. As it is, we're going locally to a place that fancies itself as an English pub. It's a far cry in reality but the food's good.'

'Then what more could we ask?' she said politely, wondering what type of restaurant he would like to take her to. Somewhere expensive? Was that what he had meant? Or. . . somewhere romantic? Guiltily she thought of Alan and what his reaction would be if he knew she had spent the entire day with an extremely attractive, talented enigma of a man who had encouraged her to tell him all about herself. Certainly he wouldn't like the idea, but—would he be outraged? Jealous? Or would he think little of it because he, he above all people, knew she could be trusted?

That last thought brought her eyes open and she turned to look at Tor, at the masculine perfection of his tanned body. She was not unaffected by his attractiveness, it was high time she acknowledged that, but there was surely nothing to worry about. It wasn't as if Tor had made a wrong move towards her; she couldn't even be sure what he thought of her as a woman. She had no idea then that by the end of the evening she would be in no doubt.

She left her brother's apartment at eight on the dot, dressed in a simple white shift that accentuated her ever-deepening suntan. Tor's suggestion that she had a pre-dinner drink in his apartment had been accepted by her readily because she was curious to see his place.

'We-ell! Aren't you looking good!' Those were his

opening words as he let her in, catching hold of her hand and adding, 'I prefer your hair down like that. It's glorious.'

Emma was quite pleased with it herself. The sun had lightened it a few shades without drying it unduly and it was loose around her shoulders in a mass of well-behaved curls.

He led her into the living-room and only then did he let go of her hand. 'What would you like to drink, Emma?'

'I'd like to look round first,' she said bluntly, her eyes taking in every detail of his living-room. It was very different from the apartment next door and it told its own story. Had she walked in here as a total stranger she might well have thought the place was inhabited by a female. There were several vases of flowers around and at least half a dozen plants. The paintings on the walls were colourful but tranquil, mostly seascapes at sunset and snow scenes in which children were playing, clad gaily in colourful clothing. They surprised Emma, though she didn't know why.

Tor's choice of furniture did not surprise her. It was predominantly Scandinavian, sleek and solid and simple. His study, his place of work, was yet a different story, however. In here the furniture was heavy; the huge desk was leather-topped and antique, as was the leather armchair in a corner.

She turned to him, feeling obliged to make some comment, only to find that he was watching her. 'I'm—you have a curious mixture of styles, Tor.'

He threw back his head and laughed delightedly. 'How very tactful! It's a hodge-podge, Emma. I know it. When

I bought the place I just didn't care—about anything. This desk and that chair, you may be surprised to learn, belonged to Pamela, my wife. They're the only things I kept from our marital home, our main home, I mean. The rest of the stuff I sold together with the house, lock, stock and barrel. I bought everything else you see in the course of one day, without any thought except that I had to have things to sit on and look at and sleep in.' The laughter faded suddenly as his eyes moved back to the antique desk. 'It's time I got rid of that, now. I kept it only because Pam was so fond of it. She liked antiques, though they never turned me on particularly. I just——' He broke off, shaking his head. 'Come on, let me get you that drink.'

He did not show her his bedroom.

Once they were in the restaurant—it was far more a restaurant than the English pub it was attempting to be—Emma declined a second drink. There would be wine with the meal and she didn't want to drink too much.

Tor teased her as she lingered over the menu. 'Now you can go to town. There's no more walking in store, so you can eat to your heart's content.'

'There's still my figure to think about.'

There was low laughter but he made no comment, not aloud at any rate. Rather he let his eyes move slowly from her face to her bare arms to her breasts, and his liking of what he saw was unmistakable.

Fixing her own eyes rigidly back on the menu, Emma wondered whether her approval of his appearance showed so clearly. He wore plain white slacks and a very pale blue open-necked shirt. No one in the restaurant wore a jacket or tie, for it was just too hot for that, but no other man looked even remotely as striking as Tor. The sleeves of his shirt were short, contrasting with the tanned length of his strong forearms. . . and where it was open at the neck she could see the attractive start of the hair on his chest. But above all else it was the blond mane, perhaps, that was his most striking feature. No, no it was his incredibly blue eyes. . .

'Emma? You haven't decided yet?'

She felt a hint of colour in her cheeks and blinked, glancing away, cross with herself at her train of thought. 'I'm—I'll have something plain and simple. Steak and salad and a baked potato.'

'The staple diet of all good Americans.' He leaned forward, catching hold of her free hand. 'And to drink? You will help me with a bottle of wine?'

She nodded. He chose a Californian red and it was excellent, better than she had expected it to be. When she said as much he laughed. 'They're not all as good, far from it. But the Californians are getting there, eventually.' He shook his head and added, 'But that's not the reason for my mirth, Emma. I'm laughing because you're so blunt—especially for an English girl. You are a curious mixture of bluntness and reserve; I find it quite fascinating.'

'And you,' she countered, emboldened, perhaps, by the wine, 'are a complete mystery to me.'

'Am I?'

'Very much so.'

'And am I to understand that you'd like to change that?'

'Very much so,' she repeated, speaking with more feeling than she had intended. 'You know all about me, Tor; won't you tell me about yourself now?'

He sobered, looking closely at her, as if he wanted to be sure she was really interested, not just making polite conversation.

'Begin by telling me about your name. Is it short for something?'

'No. Tor is it. I was named after my father.'

'You never mention your mother. Can I take it she's no longer around?'

'She died when I was three. She was English, as you know, and I have only the vaguest memory of her.'

'So your father brought you up single-handed? Have you any brothers or sisters?'

'No siblings. There would have been, according to Dad, if my mother had lived.' He straightened, sitting back in his chair to look at her, one hand idly toying with his wine glass. 'As to your other question—yes and no. My father brought me up single-handed in as much as he was a single parent. But there were a series of nannies and housekeepers and heaven knows what. There was always staff. There had to be, I saw little of my father in the early years of my life.'

He spoke lightly, evenly, but Emma detected a note of something. . . it wasn't quite resentment but. . . 'Your childhood was a lonely one?'

'Hellishly. From the age of four I was tutored privately before going to prep school, then public school, in England. My father,' he added with a shrug, 'is a very successful man. He's a lawyer, involved in corporate law, and he works on an international basis.'

'Works? Present tense?'

'Present tense. He's sixty, but he hasn't had the good sense your father had. No early retirement for him. No retirement at all. He'll work till he drops. He had a heart attack a year ago but it didn't slow him up one iota. Now there's a person who does live to work. He's a very rich man who enjoys having money just for the sake of having it. He flits around the world—from New York to London to Paris to Oslo mainly—but only because that's where his work takes him.'

Emma looked at him uncertainly, wondering whether he would answer her next question honestly. 'Do you get on with him?'

'These days, yes. Reasonably well. But in my childhood years I resented him for never being there. When I was a teenager, however, I grew to have a certain respect for him simply because he was so high-powered. I thought I wanted to be like that. He'd always told me I would be, and so—well, I began to believe it simply because I wanted to believe it. That's how I came to read law, as he had. At Harvard, as he had. By the time I was eighteen, though, I wondered why the hell I'd undertaken to study something which didn't actually appeal to me. That was when I wrote *Under the Honeysuckle*.'

She nodded, having already had the thought herself. 'So when the book proved to be a success, you gave up studying law.'

'No.' There was a cynical twist to his mouth. 'Oh, no. I carried on because I was convinced by my father that my book's success was a flash in the pan. He was scornful about it, too, telling me that writing was no way to earn a decent living. Most especially "that kind of stuff". I took it to heart and didn't attempt to write anything else for two years. And *then* I quit. I took off for Norway, which was as much home to me as England or the States, bought my own apartment in Oslo and settled down to write in earnest. My father freaked out and we didn't speak to one another for a whole year.

'One day, he called me and asked me to have dinner with him. He was at his own place in Oslo and was staying for three days. We talked, we actually communicated properly for the first time ever. I told him that law had never interested me, that I had been attempting only to mimic him. I'd realised that by then. It's so easy to take on ideas, mind-sets which aren't really our own, Emma. Everyone does to some extent or other. I'd been seeking to please him, that's all. It's an easy trap to fall into, to go along with the expectations of our parents in order to please.'

'Did you tell him this? Did you explain?'

'Yes. And he didn't argue about it. In fact he admitted how much his own father had influenced him. He said that as he'd grown older he had looked back and realised how many patterns he had followed as far as his own father's way of life was concerned. We parted friends and have been friends ever since. I don't see too much of him—but I'm near enough to fly up to New York to see him now and then, which I take the trouble to, especially since his heart attack.'

'He hasn't eased up at all since that happened?'

'Not at all.'

There was a momentary silence. Emma's mind zipped away. She was thinking about *Under the Honeysuckle*, understanding, now, a very great deal about its author. That the author of that book had known all about loneliness had always been obvious. The boy in the story, a ten-year-old who used to sit under the honeysuckle in the garden, to dream and fantasise, had been Tor himself.

She looked at him with fresh eyes, feeling a sudden closeness she couldn't quite account for.

'Emma? Where have you gone?'

'*Under the Honeysuckle,*' she said without preamble. 'You referred to writing as being a catharsis. That must have been——'

He was nodding, ahead of her. 'It was something to get out of my system. Almost everything I've written has been a coming to terms with the past, one way or another.'

It was she who reached for his hand this time, but she didn't surprise herself because she didn't notice she had done it. 'I'm sorry and yet I'm not sorry. I'm sorry your childhood was so desperately lonely—yet I can't regret the gifts which are the books you've written. Not just to children but to many adults, too. I re-read *Honeysuckle* when I was eighteen, as a matter of interest, and I got a lot from it even at that age. Probably more, because I understood more.'

Tor said nothing, he merely looked at her hand, resting on the back of his.

Emma withdrew it and tossed her hair back, feeling a little foolish. 'I'm—did your father never remarry?'

'No way! To my knowledge there hasn't been a serious relationship—nor anything remotely like it—though there have been women in his life, naturally.'

'Did he get on with your wife, Pamela?'

This brought a smile. 'He adored her, said she was good for me. Pam was American, but I met her in London, at a party. She was on vacation there. I was twenty-eight by then and we were married within three weeks of meeting. Dad knew nothing about it until two days before the wedding. He flew from Paris to be there—after lecturing me on how impulsive I was being. He ate his words later, though.'

Another silence. Emma broke it not because she was uncomfortable with it but because she simply had to ask how his wife had died. 'She must have been very young . . .'

'Twenty-seven when she died. I—we'd waited three years for her to get pregnant, and when she finally did . . .'

For a moment Emma thought he would be unable to continue; she could see him collecting himself, could see the pain in his eyes again. She almost wished she hadn't asked. 'I'm sorry, Tor, I shouldn't have——'

'It's all right.' He looked straight at her, speaking without emotion or even inflexion as he went on. 'When she died, she was six months pregnant. It was an accident. She was only out shopping. Hit and run. She was killed outright.'

'Oh, Tor!' Emma didn't know where to look, she certainly couldn't return his steady gaze. She folded her hands on the table before her and felt a disproportionate gratitude when the waiter came to enquire about desserts.

She shook her head. Even had she still felt hungry she couldn't have eaten anything else. She felt sick, stunned at the idea of Pamela being killed like that. . . and six months pregnant! Dear heaven, how had Tor survived it? How had he coped with such a loss? Not only his beloved wife but also his much-wanted child, the baby which had been so close to becoming a person in its own right.

'Nothing for me, either, thanks. What about coffee, Emma?'

She declined that, too, but Tor ordered some, and when

the waiter had gone, he said quietly, 'One side-effect of that. . . experience. . . was that it gave me a better understanding of my father. I was able to understand, really to understand, how he had felt when my mother had died. Until then I'd had only an intellectual appreciation. He was very supportive, and for that I'll always be grateful.'

'Beware,' she said, equally quietly, unable to stop herself, 'that you don't fall into the mimicry trap again.'

He looked at her sharply, a frown pulling his blond brows together. 'What do you mean?'

Emma took a deep breath, but she had to say it. 'Well, I'm only guessing but—isn't it possible that part of your father's driving himself so hard is, or was, due to the loss of his wife?'

'It isn't merely possible, it's probable. So?'

'So your reaction has been different. You stopped caring, about anything. I quote. You didn't care where you lived and you didn't care about your surroundings, I mean the things around you in your home. And almost three years later, that's still the case.' The intensity in his eyes did not put her off; on the contrary, it encouraged her because he was looking at her with a keen interest, in a way he had never looked at her before. 'Tor, all I'm saying is that it doesn't have to be the same for you. Your father never remarried, he hasn't even had a serious relationship to your knowledge, but it doesn't have to be the same for you. And there is a danger of it, isn't there?'

'I don't see it as a danger, Emma——'

'You wanted children. You're thirty-four years old, you're still young, yet you told me the other night that you're not looking for any sort of permanent relationship.

Why is that?'

'Hey, come on!' He laughed a little, trying to lighten the mood. 'I'm far from being unhappy, lovely one. I've come to terms with Pamela's death and I'm enjoying life again, really I am. And I take life as it comes, Emma, with the attitude that what will be will be.'

A sudden bout of laughter from the next table distracted her momentarily and when she turned back to Tor, it was to see him smiling, leaning towards her to make some comment about the people who were laughing. She listened, smiling also, but she did not actually register what he was saying because her mind was still on their previous conversation—a conversation which was clearly finished now. Had she been too presumptuous? Too personal? If so, she didn't care. She had meant what she'd said—and she didn't believe for one minute that Tor was as happy as he purported to be. Nor did she believe that he would take life as it came to him, any more than she believed he was over Pamela's death. Whether he knew it or not, he had built an invisible wall against the prospect of getting seriously involved again with any woman.

She said no more, and when he carried on talking to her in a lighter vein she flowed with it, laughing genuinely when he went on to tell her about his first experience of being drunk—at the age of thirteen—a story prompted by the fact that two of the party on the next table had obviously had far too much.

'I wasn't quite so young, I was fifteen.' She turned to him laughingly as they crossed the car park and got into his Oldsmobile. 'And we got drunk on a bottle of sherry, would you believe? Cooking sherry at that!'

'We? You and David?'

'No, no!' The idea of that made her laugh more. 'Not David! He was far too serious about things even at fifteen. All he was interested in at that age was his schoolwork. No, I got drunk with a girl called Christine Connolly. She was something of a ringleader at school, rather forward, as my mother used to refer to her, and we clubbed together to buy this bottle of sherry. Boy, did I have a headache the next day . . . and the day after! I didn't taste alcohol of any sort again until my eighteenth birthday.'

'I believe it!'

They were still laughing when they emerged from the elevator on the third floor of their building. 'How about a nightcap now?' Tor spoke with mischief in his eyes, his arm moving to drape casually around her shoulder. 'I don't think there's any cooking sherry in my apartment but I have got a bottle of fine French brandy. If you——'

'Thank you, but no.' She interrupted him, her answer coming too swiftly, too stiffly, and when he turned to look at her this time, it was with slightly narrowed eyes.

'No, Emma? But what's your hurry?'

'There's no hurry, I just—want to see that David's OK.' It wasn't true, and David was the last thing on her mind. She just didn't want to be alone with Tor, not in the privacy of his apartment.

And he knew it, she realised, as he gathered her into his arms regardless. 'What's the matter, Emma, don't you trust me? Or is it yourself you don't trust?'

There was only one way she could react, with as much indignation as she could find. She had to hide her thoughts, her feelings, the fact that his touch, casual though it was, was sending a delicious warmth through her entire body. 'And what's that supposed to mean? I don't understand you, Tor.'

He merely laughed at that, taking hold of her arms with both hands. 'I think you understand me very well. You know very well what it means, and you know very well how attractive I find you, too. Just as you know I've been wanting for the past few hours to take you in my arms and kiss you.'

No, she had not known that. Had she? Or had she ignored the realisation, just as she had ignored from day one how very attractive he was to her?

She glanced away, unable to meet those incredibly blue eyes any longer. 'Please, I don't want to hear this. Don't spoil everything——'

'*Spoil* everything? Emma——'

'Don't!' She wrenched away from him, reminding him coldly that she was engaged. 'I'm going to marry Alan Dobson in the spring, kindly remember that!'

'You're certainly not going to let me forget it, are you?' The roughness in her voice shocked her and she turned back to face him at the precise moment he reached for her. The next thing she knew was that she was enfolded in his arms, hard up against his body, and his mouth came down on hers determinedly. She fought, twisting her head away frantically, as if a solitary kiss from Tor Pedersen might have the power to change how she felt about Alan, to change all the plans she had for her future.

That his kiss might just do that was a chance she was not prepared to take, so she continued to struggle until he let her go, his low laughter following her as she fled into the safety of the apartment next door.

CHAPTER FIVE

'GOOD morning, Emma. How are you today?'

She turned wearily to look at her brother, dismayed to see him looking as pale as he had been this time last week. 'OK. You can't say the same, though, can you? You stayed up too late last night.'

She was a fine one to talk; hour upon hour had dragged by before sleep had claimed her the previous night. She had lain awake thinking about Alan and about Tor. Why, she had no idea. She knew only that there was no comparison between the two men, they were different from one another in every possible way—and yet she *had* been comparing them. Why? What had been the point in doing that?

She turned back to the window at which she had been standing for the past half-hour, watching Tor swimming relentlessly, length after length. It was difficult not to watch him, difficult to take her eyes from his strong, graceful body as he cut through the water, his tanned skin glinting in the morning sun.

'Did you hear me, Emma? I said Alan phoned again last night.'

'At what time?' she asked, feeling her heart sink. 'Do you remember what time it was?'

'Of course I do. Nine-fifteen exactly. Which means——'

'Which means it was two-fifteen in the morning in England.'

'Quite. He was a bit smashed, I think. I wasn't sure how to explain your absence so I told him you were fed up with staying in and had gone to the flicks. I thought it better not to say——'

'You were wrong. You should have told him the truth.' There was defiance in her eyes, in her voice, though she didn't realise to what extent. 'I have nothing to hide. And where the devil had he been anyway? If it was two in the morning, he'd probably just come in from a night on the town.'

David opened his mouth to say something, thought better of it and headed for the kitchen instead. 'I'll put the coffee on.'

'I'll do it. You go back to bed, you look shattered.'

'I might look shattered, but I'm not feeling it, oddly enough. I'm all right. Anyhow,' he added, glancing at his watch, 'Anna should be here in about half an hour.'

'She's coming again?' The words were out before Emma had time to think what she was saying. It had sounded like a protest, but it wasn't really. What right would she have to protest? David was not a child, he was twenty-four years old and this was his apartment.

'Certainly. It's Sunday and she's free. Why shouldn't she come again?'

'I'm—of course she should. I just wasn't thinking, that's all.' As he moved towards the kitchen, she turned back to the window—only to discover that Tor was no longer in the pool.

When the doorbell rang a few minutes later, she hardly knew what to do with herself. David had disappeared into the bathroom, leaving her no option but to open the door herself. But she didn't want to face Tor, not yet, not until she'd had time to compose herself, to put last night into perspective. Oh, not just the last five minutes of it but *all* of it. The entire evening had had an effect on her, and she had not yet sorted out what that effect had been, exactly.

On the one hand she felt angry with him, on the other hand she felt she had grown to know him better than she knew her own fiancé. She knew that was crazy, she knew it couldn't really be so, but that was what it felt like. This, within the space of one day, albeit a long and glorious day. But *one day* of his company none the less. It made a mockery of something she had been sure of earlier in the week, when she had thought him complex and full of contradictions, when she had told herself she could never get to know him if she lived next door to him for three years!

Still, she had to face him some time, and when the doorbell rang for a second time, David's voice came very loudly from the bathroom. 'Answer it, Emma! It's Anna, she's early.'

But it wasn't Anna, as Emma already knew; it was Tor. A colourful beach towel was slung around his neck and his denim shorts had been pulled on over his swimming-trunks. 'Good morning, Emma. And a glorious one it is, too! How're you today?'

She stepped back, gesturing him to come inside, knowing a profound sense of relief at his naturalness. As far as he was concerned, nothing had changed between them. 'Morning, Tor. I'm fine, thanks. Coffee's almost perked—will you have a cup?'

'I'd love one. Is David up yet? I saw you were, saw you from downstairs.'

'David's in the bathroom. He's expecting Anna any

time now.'

'I see.' There was a rumble of laughter which brought her eyes to his. 'Do you suppose they might be interested in a trip up the river?'

'Up the river?'

He laughed again at that. 'You know, that big blue wet thing out there? I have a speedboat in the marina. Does that sort of thing appeal to you?'

Did it ever! 'I can't speak for David and Anna, but——'

'What's up?' David appeared, looking pleased, as ever, to see his neighbour. 'How are you doing, Tor? Planning to whisk my sister away again, are you?'

'I'd like to whisk us all away, if you're game, David. I hear Anna's coming. Must be a devil for punishment, that girl. Do you think she'd like to spend a couple of hours on the James this morning?'

'I dare say she might, but it would kill me. Sorry, any other time I'd say yes, but I'm not up to that just yet.'

A dozen thoughts zipped through Emma's mind in rapid succession. There was no way Anna would go without David, of course, so what was she herself going to say? The invitation would still be open to her—she didn't doubt that—but should she accept it? Heavens, it was tempting! Her eyes flitted briefly to the blue sky, the sunlight streaming in, and she could think of no nicer way of spending the morning than sailing at high speed along the James River with Tor. Most especially with Tor.

She shouldn't go.

He might deem it encouragement and, in any case, she planned to telephone Alan today. It didn't matter what time she phoned him, exactly, as long as she got him before he took the train back to Winchester tonight. He might well have gone to London by car, in which case he would drive back early Monday morning.

She became aware of Tor looking at her, aware of his words: 'It looks as though it'll be just you and me, then.'

For just a moment she hesitated. Had he spoken with any hint of satisfaction, any hint that this was what he had wanted and had known all along would be the case, she would have refused. Definitely. But the face she was looking at was impassive, his tone nothing but neutral. So how could she refuse, really? She couldn't, not without seeming contrary. Nor, in honesty, did she want to. But she did intend to make one point, and about that she did not hesitate. 'Give me half an hour, would you? I want to have a chat to my fiancé and if I'm going out I must change into something cooler.'

It got a reaction, albeit one she could have kicked him for. The blue eyes settled steadily on hers and he said with exaggerated acquiescence, 'But of course. By all means take time to chat to your fiancé first. Take as long as you like, Emma. Why limit yourself to half an hour? Just knock on my door when you're ready, I'm not going anywhere.'

Half an hour later she did just that, fully prepared for him to quiz her. He didn't. He did not ask about her exchange with Alan, he didn't make any reference to it at all. Instead he looked her over from top to toe, his eyes taking in every detail from the curls of her ponytail hairstyle to the expanse of bare midriff between her emerald green shorts and matching top, down to the teak-coloured sandals on her feet.

'Tor...' The word came from her unwillingly, a protest she would have preferred not to make. But it was necessary because he was looking at her body with such flagrant, deliberate appreciation that it provoked a response in her. She felt as if she had been touched by him, caressed by him, and it disturbed her more than she would admit even to herself. 'Stop it, Tor!' It came sharply, so she went on quickly, attempting to add a splash of humour, 'The lady is not amused.'

'The lady,' he countered swiftly, with not even a hint of humour, 'is not immune, either, no matter what she would have me believe.'

Tearing along a river under the rays of scorching sunshine was an unprecedented and wildly exhilarating experience for Emma. She had given up on her ponytail within the first five minutes, had stuffed the ponytail ring into her pocket and let her hair fly free and frantic in the wind. There were moments when breathing was quite difficult, and she gasped in delight as the boat slammed against the surface of the water, rising and falling, zipping along at a rate she would not have believed possible, having no experience of speedboats.

Conversation at anything less than a scream was impossible, despite her physical nearness to Tor at the controls. When at last he eased up and finally cut the engine, she was breathless and disorientated both.

He laughed. 'You *seemed* to like it.'

'Like it?' Emma laughed uproariously, excited in a way she had never been excited before. 'I loved it, *loved* it!'

And then it happened. She turned with the intention of sitting down, misjudged her footing and started to fall. Tor's arms came around her instantly and she was hauled unceremoniously back on her feet, gasping out her thanks as her hands moved to cover his, to remove his, from the bare skin of her midriff. Except that it didn't work that way. She was turned around within the circle of one arm and he took full advantage of the moist, open invitation that was her mouth.

Her protest died in her throat. He had caught her at precisely the right instant, when she was exquisitely vulnerable, still disorientated and struggling to breathe normally. And so his kiss was gentle, in no way hindering her breathing, and it was perhaps because of his gentleness that she made no effort to break free from him.

A moment later she was free of him, but only because he had raised his head to look into her eyes. Unconsciously her fingers moved to touch her lips, to feel where his mouth had been, gentle but persistent, on hers.

When he moved infinitesimally towards her again she stepped back smartly, uncaring of the rocking of the boat. 'No!'

'Oh, yes,' he said softly. But he didn't move. Instead he repeated himself, his eyes smiling gently and knowingly into hers, knowingly but without triumph. 'Oh, yes, Emma. But next time, you will kiss me.'

By four o'clock they were lying on the beautiful white sand of Virginia Beach, having stuffed themselves a short time earlier with pizzas. It had taken just an hour to drive here from the apartment and Emma was still telling herself that she had extended her time with Tor for two reasons. Firstly, Anna had somehow persuaded David to sit in the sun for a while—and the pair had been found by the pool on Emma's return from the river. Secondly, she had told Alan that she was going out with David's neighbour. He hadn't minded at all. At least, he hadn't said he minded.

'Is that the bloke who was in there when I phoned the other day?' This was about all he had asked, except for 'A friend of David's, is he?'

'Yes, he is.' Emma had left it at that, assuming Alan would think no more about it, now he knew that the man was a friend as well as a neighbour.

Now, however, she felt swamped with guilt. The incident on the boat kept coming back to haunt her, as did Tor's words. 'But next time, you will kiss me.'

Irrelevant. There wouldn't be a next time, one way or another, because she was going to make it her business not to be alone again with Tor in a place that was private or even semi-private, not after today.

'You've been very quiet since our ride on the river, Emma. Is something bothering you?'

She turned quickly to look at him, thinking again that he was too perceptive, that it was no coincidence that he was asking her this question right now, when she was indeed feeling bothered, extremely so. 'Nothing at all,' she lied, wishing his eyes were open so that she could look into them and get an idea of what he was thinking.

He told her what he was thinking. 'You're lying,' he said.

Pointlessly she stared at him, fascinated by and almost resentful of his rugged handsomeness. 'I haven't the faintest idea what you're talking about.'

And still his eyes remained closed. 'You have every idea. Do you think I was unaware of your response when I kissed you earlier? Why is it bugging you so much? Why are you sitting there fidgeting and feeling guilty about it? I'm picking up your vibes, they're crawling all over me. Why don't you lie back and relax? Denying the attraction between us is not going to make it disappear.'

She turned her head away, knowing that to lie further would be pointless. But how could he read her so well, so accurately? And why, at some deeper level she was not prepared to investigate, did she find his accurate understanding of her exciting? It was perverse; *she* was being perverse. 'Can we go back?' she blurted out suddenly. 'I—think I've had enough sun for today.'

Tor didn't argue, he simply got to his feet and they started gathering their belongings together. They were in any case due back by seven because Anna was cooking dinner for the four of them.

It was at some point during the middle of the meal that evening that David mentioned Anna's having a week's vacation due. Realising at once what this would mean, Emma looked at the other girl, hoping her question sounded casual. 'This week? Do you mean this week, Anna, or next week?'

'Sorry. Next week. Today's Sunday, isn't it? You're quite right, David should have said next week.'

There was an exchange of smiles but Emma barely noticed. She was preoccupied, focused now on the reality of going back to England. Anna wasn't going away somewhere; she would be around—which meant she would be around this apartment to look after David. That had been implicitly understood by everyone. So where did that leave Emma? Redundant. No longer needed. One more week here and she could go home, leaving her brother in the very capable hands of the girl he would one day marry.

At eleven o'clock she excused herself, thanked Anna for her hard work in the kitchen, and Tor for a lovely day, and escaped to her bedroom for some much-needed privacy. She needed to think, needed to sort out why she was not filled with enthusiasm at the prospect of going home. It would be wonderful to see Alan again, and it would feel good to be back at work. And her father—well, he would be glad to get back to his normal routine with his wife. There was every good reason in the world for going home.

The sound of the outer door closing and, a moment later, the sound of the door closing in the next apartment told her that Tor had taken his leave. Fifteen minutes after that Anna left, and David spent five noisy minutes in the bathroom. Emma turned over in bed and wondered why her brother always managed to make so much noise during the simple act of brushing his teeth.

She had to face it. Tor Pedersen was the problem. The prospect of never seeing him again was an unwelcome one, that was the top and bottom of it. Well, it wouldn't do, it was too ridiculous, and from now on she would avoid him like the plague—before she began to like him too much, perhaps, for her own good.

The crash of thunder woke her at two minutes past two. What warning there had been of the storm's approach she had no idea, for she woke with a tremendous start right in the middle of it. Unperturbed, she got out of bed, pulled on jeans and a sweatshirt and acknowledged with a smile that what she was about to do would be regarded as madness by a lot of people, David included.

A moment later she was sitting on his unlit balcony, uncaring that she was only partially protected from the downpour. The rain fell in sheets, so thick and fast that the spray of it encircled her where she sat on the shallow concrete platform. She didn't even hear her brother's approach, the opening of the sliding glass door behind her.

'Are you absolutely nutty, Emma Browning?'

She didn't turn to look at him, she just laughed at him. 'Throw some clothes on. Come out here and share this with me. You know I've always loved storms. I've never seen a tropical storm before.'

'Tropical—really, Emma, if you must romanticise, don't expect me to feel the same way. I don't happen to like storms, remember?'

'Were you scared? Is that why you came looking for me?'

'Oh, shut up. If you must experience this from outside the building, then at least save yourself a drenching and go outside, right outside. You'd be better off downstairs, under the awning, at least it's a windbreak and——'

She was already on her feet, wondering why she hadn't thought of it herself. 'Don't wait up, I'll take my keys!'

It was perfect. By skirting closely around the building she had been able to reach the shelter of the very wide, very deep, scarlet awning without getting soaked. Apart from the white tables and chairs that were always here, sun-loungers had been stacked and there were several two-seater hammocks with comfortable cushions. Emma had opted for one of those and was now sitting, swinging gently, with her eyes fixed on the awesome drama of the lightning shooting raggedly across the sky.

The temperature had dropped but not by much; it was comfortable and the air smelt gloriously fresh. She stood for a moment in order to look across the river and, in the foreground, at the boats in the marina as they bobbed on the water's surface.

The sound of a voice behind her was shocking, so unexpected that she spun round too quickly, half falling back on to the hammock. 'Good grief! You nearly frightened the life out of me! What are you doing out here, Tor? Are you——'

'As fond of storms as you, apparently.'

'I've always found them exciting . . .' Her voice trailed off when he moved with his effortless grace to sit beside her. Quite suddenly she was tongue-tied, not knowing what else to say.

But there was nothing else to say. Tor settled himself and the seat swung back and forth for a moment before steadying, at which point he took hold of her hand and looked towards the heavens. Emma followed his gaze, enjoying as he was the moon's game as it appeared and disappeared in the rolling black clouds. There was no let-up in the downpour, the rain battered the surrounding grounds and the water of the swimming pool with a vengeance while the two spectators sat in silence, absorbing the scene. Behind them the external lights of the apartment building were puny to the point where they were not noticeable until suddenly they went out. Within a minute they flickered on again, but neither Tor nor Emma remarked on it.

How long they sat like that, motionless and silent, she could never be sure afterwards. Five minutes? Fifteen? Anyway, the storm continued to rage directly above them and had she not turned at some point fleetingly to glance at Tor, their shared experience might have ended very differently. It might have ended, with the end of the storm or at least its moving on, with a simple goodnight and a shared smile. But turn to him she did, and in that single second she saw this man, she *knew* this man, as she had never apprehended him before. It was beyond a logical explanation: it was a recognition she could not begin to understand. It just was. In a solitary glance at his profile, at the eyes lit briefly by a flash of blue-white lightning, it seemed to Emma that she knew him more intimately than she knew her own twin brother. The recognition, the understanding, came in snatches as brief as the flashes of lightning, and yet there was nothing missing from the wholeness of what she knew. It was like having an overview of the entirety of him. Tor Pedersen, motherless, a lonely child, wanting and needing his father's presence. Denied his father's presence. Grudgingly learning in time a respect for the parent he had resented and, believing he should follow in father's footsteps, pushing himself into a mould he could never fit. No one country had been home, but several had been, or so he believed. And then there was Pamela. There was stability, marriage, the prospect of children and permanence and . . . and then she was killed. Killed senselessly, pregnant with the child he, they, had wanted so much.

All the knowingness was there in one fleeting moment. That, and more, for she knew also that the man she was looking at now was every bit as lonely as the child who had sat under the honeysuckle.

Did he realise it himself? Did he realise the true extent of it? It pained her; without warning her heart lurched agonisingly, and his name came involuntarily to her lips. 'Tor . . .' Even as she spoke, she was reaching for him. There was time only for her to register the look of surprise on his face and then she was kissing him fully on the mouth, fully but tenderly, as if she would erase all she had seen in that strange solitary second.

Tor's response was equally tender. His arms came around her gently and she parted her lips beneath the light pressure of his mouth. For minutes they kissed like that, their mouths separating only to touch elsewhere, on cheeks, on closed eyelids, before coming together again, before going on to communicate in a way that words never could.

Oddly, Emma was aware of no sound, no rainfall, no storm, but she did hear her own soft gasp when Tor's lips moved to trace a line from the base of her ear down the side of her neck to her throat. There they nestled against the pulse-point while her arms tightened around him in encouragement.

He gathered her in closer, making her aware of the hard wall of his chest against her breasts. When his lips moved to the side of her neck at her shoulder she held him more tightly and, as if he knew precisely what she wanted, he bit gently into the soft flesh there, drawing from her a little moan, an invitation.

Then her name was on Tor's lips and he spoke against her mouth. Again she took the initiative, moving fractionally so they were joined once again. But this time it was different, this time he explored the softness of her mouth with a hungry tongue, probing and testing, tasting, drawing from her a response she had not known herself capable of. The desire which had begun so tremulously in her took hold in earnest to the point where she was suddenly consumed by it, her entire body yearning towards him.

'I want you. Emma, I want you so much . . .'

She heard the words and she silently acquiesced, yet at the touch of his hand beneath her shirt, at the warm caress of her breast, at the feeling of flesh against flesh so intimate, something in her recoiled and this time she gasped in shock.

Alan! The name reverberated inside her head like a ricocheting bullet.

Blankly she stared for an instant at the face so close to hers, a face so familiar but—wrong! It was the wrong face, the wrong man. 'I . . .' That was as far as she got; communication of any kind had become impossible. How could she explain that this was all a mistake? How could she tell him she had never felt like this before, not in the arms of any man, even those of her fiancé? And how could she tell him it almost terrified her, that she was dreadfully sorry this had happened? 'I'm sorry—so very sorry, Tor.' It was all she could manage and it was pathetic, she knew that. But her mind was reeling in confusion, reeling with questions neither of them would be able to answer. How could this have happened? How could she have responded like this, behaved like this, when she was engaged to someone else?

'Wait.' The word came when she made a move to escape from Tor. It came softly, so softly she could not fail to hear the danger in it. His hand encircled her wrist in a steel-hard grip and she stayed where she was, rigidly still, her head averted. 'Look at me,' he commanded. 'I said look at me, Emma.'

'I can't.' It was a whisper. 'I can't bear your anger.'

'I'm not angry, I'm disappointed.'

'I'm sorry, I know it was at my——'

'I don't mean that, I mean I'm disappointed in you. I thought you were more honest. This time——'

'Then let me be honest,' she cut in, turning to meet his eyes with a defiance she was not aware of. 'I simply don't know what happened just now. It was—I am engaged to be married and I——'

'Oh, I know all about *that*, do I not? Haven't you taken care constantly to remind me of it? You've been holding up your status and that precious engagement ring like a crucifix to a vampire! Can't you see——'

'It didn't stop you, though, did it?' Angrily she tried in vain to get her arm free. 'A fat lot of respect you've shown for my status, as you put it!'

'About as much as you yourself have shown.' Again his words came quietly but they struck home, they struck to the point where Emma had to avert her head for fear he might see the threat of tears in her eyes. Inwardly she acknowledged she deserved that remark, that it was accurate. What had happened tonight had been at her instigation; she had acted as if she were free to behave as she wished with another man. Outwardly, however, she attacked Tor, resenting his remark regardless of its accuracy. 'How dare you judge me? You don't know me. You can't begin to understand how I feel about——'

'But I do know you, Emma.' The words were spoken so softly that they were barely audible this time. 'You'd be surprised, staggered, if you knew how very well I understand and know you.'

She closed her eyes against the words, determined not to acknowledge them. No, she would not be staggered, not even surprised, because the same thing had happened to her, and the one idea paramount in her mind now was that it wasn't at all like this with herself and Alan. There was something missing in her relationship with her fiancé and she was forced, now, to acknowledge that fact. 'Tor, I want to go inside now.'

'You're going nowhere. I have something else to say.'

In the momentary silence which followed, Emma looked around, wanting to avoid those very perceptive eyes of his. The rain had eased off to a mere trickle. All was still, all was quiet except for the low rumble of thunder, far in the distance now. She looked up and saw the moon peeping from behind a cloud, feeling very aware of her unsteady heartbeat, very aware of Tor.

'As I began to say earlier, Emma, can't you see that there's something missing in your relationship with Alan? If this weren't the case, you wouldn't be feeling towards me the way you do.'

She laughed, a nervous, tense little noise with no mirth in it. He was not telling her something new; she had realised for herself that all was not as it should be with Alan, but she had only just realised it and she didn't yet know what she was going to do about it. And she was damned if she was going to discuss this, any of it, with Tor Pedersen. So it was with cynicism and coldness that she began to answer him. 'Talk about the male ego! Do you——'

'No.' He shook his head almost wearily. 'No, that's too easy to say and it doesn't wash. I'm not that insecure, Emma, I don't need to make a conquest of you in order to satisfy my ego.' With his free hand he caught hold of her chin, turning her head so she was obliged to look at him. To her amazement he was grinning. 'My body, yes, but not my ego.'

Emma wouldn't smile, she could not smile. 'Will you please let go of me, let go of my wrist? I have nothing else to say to you. I can't begin to understand what you want of me.'

'I want nothing of you.'

'Nothing?'

'I thought we were friends.'

'You thought we——' She stared at him, feeling, now, that she didn't begin to know him. Had she been reading him wrongly, quite wrongly, all along the line? It didn't seem possible but . . . 'You know, I can't decide whether you're the most devious of seducers. Don't laugh at me like that! You didn't marry until you were twenty-eight, you must have had hundreds of women. And what do I know? I admit it, I might be way out of my depth——'

'You might,' he interrupted, making no attempt to stifle his smile, 'be getting well and truly carried away. You think I'm trying to undermine you? Plotting a scheme of seduction? Come on, Emma! Give us both some credit. Your instincts can't be that far out, and I happen to believe in your instincts almost as strongly as I believe in my own.'

'Do you now?' she asked, her voice dripping sarcasm.

'Then you'd better tune in a little more strongly.' Pointedly she looked at her wrist, at the hold he still had on her. 'And perhaps you'll realise that you are holding me here against my will.'

He released her at once, but not without smiling again. Carelessly he shrugged. 'OK. Run along, if you must. I've said what I wanted to say.'

She didn't run, though it was tempting because she wanted to get away from him as quickly as possible. She needed time to think—about herself, about Alan, about what she could do to improve things between them.

CHAPTER SIX

EMMA replaced the telephone receiver with a heartfelt sigh. She had just dealt with the matter of getting her seat on a flight back to England, and the relief of knowing when she was leaving, how quickly she was leaving, was enormous. She wanted to talk to Alan, to have a long talk to Alan, just as quickly as she could. Ridiculous though it might seem at this stage, she wanted to get to know him better.

She wanted to make things *right* between them, perfect between them. Then they would set a date for their wedding. It was time they set a date now, rather than referring to some nebulous point in the future. Besides, they would need time to make all the arrangements necessary for a big white wedding, the whole bit. The kind of wedding she had always wanted.

'Well?' David lowered his book and looked at her. He had been treating her cautiously this morning, sensing her changing moods. She had seemed cross earlier, she had rambled incoherently about Tor, saying something about his being outside in the storm last night. She hadn't made much sense; David couldn't make out whether they had fought—nor was he inclined to ask just now.

'Tomorrow, David. I leave Norfolk for New York at three-fifteen, New York for London at seven-fifty.'

'*Tomorrow*? But——'

'Just a minute.' Emma held up a hand, realising her brother had not anticipated her leaving quite so soon. But he would cope, he had insisted he could cope perfectly,

and she just had to get away. 'I'll talk to you in a minute,
I must ring Alan straight away. I want him to come for
me at Heathrow.'

'Will he be able to? Can he get time off?'

She was already dialling. 'Of course he can get time
off, he can say he's seeing a customer if needs be.'

This provoked a look of disapproval but Emma
ignored it. Her concern for the moment was getting hold
of her fiancé, hoping he was in the office. He was. Not
only that, he was wildly enthusiastic at the news of her
coming home. With a satisfied smile she put down the
receiver and told her brother of Alan's reaction.

'Well, what else did you expect? The man's in love
with you, isn't he?'

'Right on, brother!' Laughing, she leapt to her feet to
put the kettle on. 'Like some coffee?'

'I'd prefer tea myself,' he said.

It wasn't until she was on the plane back to London that
Emma wept, just briefly. She wept because it had been
difficult to part from David. Being with him had been so
nice; she loved him very dearly, different though he was
from her.

But there was a little more to it than that. If she were
totally honest, she had to admit that the prospect of never
seeing Tor again was not a welcome one. The man had
got under her skin—to the point where she had
deliberately avoided saying goodbye to him. She had seen
nothing of him since the night of the storm. Yesterday she
had packed her suitcases, hoping against hope he would
not drop in—which he hadn't. Nor had he been out at the
pool this morning. He had no idea about her rapid
departure, and she could not deny a curiosity as to what

his reaction would be when he found out. Nor could she deny that her cowardly avoidance of him had left a bad taste in her mouth. She should have steeled herself for that scene, if only for the sake of common courtesy. He had, after all, been more than hospitable to her.

'Are you all right?' The concerned voice of the stewardess broke into her thoughts. Her fellow passengers had been tactfully ignoring her weeping but the stewardess wasn't going to do that. 'Are you feeling ill?'

'No, no. I just—said goodbye to someone I won't see for a while.' Emma manufactured a smile for the woman, not bothering to lie or make excuses. Why should she? 'You know how it is.'

'Ah!' The eyes of the other woman lit on Emma's diamond engagement ring and she nodded knowingly. 'Engaged to an American, are you?'

'No! I was referring to my brother, actually.'

Left in peace again, she tried to pull herself together, to anticipate how she would actually feel on seeing Alan again. It felt as though she had been in Virginia for months, but in reality it had been only two weeks. Yet she was different. A humourless smile touched her lips. A lot could happen in the space of two weeks. A lot could happen in one day . . . she amended her thinking when recalling that long and glorious day with Tor in Richmond and in Williamsburg. How marvellous that had been! They had shared a great deal of laughter, quite apart from anything else, and . . . well, thinking about it was pointless. It was just a pity that their friendship had finished on a sour note, without the proper farewell, thanks to her.

Sleep evaded her. She was one of those people who never could sleep properly on a plane. The in-flight movie was one she had already seen with Alan, and the book she had bought in the airport couldn't hold her attention. So it was a long and boring flight, seven hours during which she felt as if she were in suspended animation, neither in one place nor another.

Alan was not there to meet her. As she emerged from the Customs hall in Heathrow Airport, Emma spotted the beloved faces of her parents almost immediately. An explanation was forthcoming as soon as hugs and kisses had been exchanged.

'Alan rang me at the shop, late afternoon yesterday,' her father began. 'Something had come up at work and he had to be in the office at eight o'clock this morning. He sends his love, his apologies and more love,' he added with a smile. 'He said he'll see you at the flat around six this evening, he won't ring before then because he expects you'll be sleeping this afternoon.'

It was now eight-fifteen in the morning, English time, though as far as Emma's body was concerned it was the middle of the night. 'I expect I'll be sleeping all day.'

'You didn't sleep on the plane, darling?' This came from her mother, who was looking bright-eyed, happy and, as ever, far younger than her fifty-six years.

'I never do, Mum.' She smiled, reaching to hug her mother for a second time. 'You look super, as always. Smart as a whip.'

'And as pretty as ever.' Jim Browning put his arm around his wife's shoulders briefly before gathering Emma's belongings on to a trolley. 'Come on, let's get this show on the road.'

'You left the keys of the shop with Madeline, Dad?'

'Of course. She's a good girl, that.'

Emma nodded. Madeline was one of her two employees, a forty-year-old 'girl' who did most of the deliveries and was a competent florist to boot.

'Now, you two. Before you start talking shop, I want a full report from Emma about David. How is he? Has he made friends over there? What's his apartment like? What are his neighbours like? Are they friendly—did you meet any of them?'

All of Iris Browning's questions were answered during the hour it took to drive to Winchester. Emma was also brought up to date on family news, the most important of which was that her sister Janice was very well and as big as a house with the twins she was expecting soon.

'She's going to have her hands full,' Jim put in, 'with twins and two others to look after. I can see you coming out of retirement for a while, Iris!'

After several cups of tea in Emma's flat, her father went down to work in the shop for this, his last day, and Iris Browning unpacked Emma's suitcases for her. 'If you want to go off to bed, darling, I'll sort your clothes and put the first batch into the washing machine. All right?'

'Thanks, Mum.' Gratefully, Emma went to bed and fell sound asleep at once. Her last waking thought was of Alan, which reminded her to set her alarm clock for four so she could be bathed and dressed for his arrival around six.

He came at ten past, letting himself in by the separate back entrance to the flat with the key Emma had given to him a couple of months earlier. Her nervousness as she heard him coming up the stairs surprised her. She had taken pains with her make-up and her hair, and she caught herself quickly checking her appearance in the mirror.

And then he was there, in the doorway, his arms held wide open to her. 'Emma! Darling, I've missed you so much, I can't tell you.'

But it didn't ring true! In the second that she paused before moving into his arms, she registered at once that something, somehow, was not right. Quite apart from that, she was taken aback because in her absence her fiancé had grown a moustache.

'Hey, what's all this?' Gently she tugged at it as she moved into his embrace, laughing because she was unsure whether or not she liked it. Alan had always been clothes-conscious, a snappy dresser, some would say, but this new addition seemed to make him look . . . flashy.

'Kiss me,' he was saying laughingly. 'See how it feels before you pass an opinion!'

Willingly she turned her face up, and he kissed her hungrily. It was a demonstration of how much he had missed her . . . and it was during the kiss that she knew, suddenly and with absolute certainty, that she could not marry him. Not in the spring, not at any time.

A whole gamut of emotions flooded through her. There was dismay, there was the dread of having to tell Alan . . . but there was a curious absence of shock. She had known. She had *known*. For a long time, deep down inside, she had known that she would never get as far as the altar with Alan Dobson. So why hadn't she faced it before? Why had she not allowed it into her consciousness? Had she been hoping the situation would change, that Alan would change?

Of course she had. Only twenty-four hours

ago—less—she had planned herself to change things, to improve this relationship. But it couldn't be improved, there was too much missing from it. There was not only the absence of that necessary depth of understanding between them, there was also the physical side of things.

Tor. Even now, as Alan's mouth was devouring hers hungrily, she could not prevent herself from thinking of Tor. Irrationally she cursed him silently for the physical response he had provoked in her.

Alan couldn't do that. Not any more. She had never responded to him with half the passion she had felt for Tor in any case. But she felt nothing now. His kiss was pleasant, and that was all. Somehow, somewhere in time, what desire she had known for Alan had died.

'Emma? What is it?'

She looked away, anticipating the most difficult time of her entire life. 'I—have to talk to you, Alan.'

He nodded, deadly serious, and moved away from her to sit on the settee. Emma sat in the armchair at a right angle to it, her hands clasped tightly in her lap. 'That's good,' he said, 'because I have to talk to you, too.'

Relief flooded her, her head came up and she looked straight into his eyes. Did he know? Did he know it was over between them? Had he, too, known it for some time, deep down inside? 'About what?' she asked cautiously.

'About us, partly. About my work, mainly.' Clearly ill at ease, he got to his feet and moved around. It was seconds before he turned to look at her. 'Emma, I'm being transferred to the London office and, while London is in commuting distance I don't want to commute.'

'You mean you want to live there.'

'I always have, you know that.'

She nodded. 'So what's your problem?'

He blinked, surprised. 'It seems there isn't one. I thought you'd go up the wall.'

'No.' Even several weeks ago her response would not have been an angry one. Winchester to London was only an hour by car, and she liked the city very much. Actually living in it didn't appeal, but they could easily have compromised on that. Had they married they could have lived on the outskirts of London, with the countryside in arm's reach, the best of both worlds.

But they were not going to be married.

She drew a deep breath. 'Alan, please tell me something, answer me honestly. Did you ask to be transferred?'

He looked sheepish. 'Yes. You know my ambitions are——'

'That's all right, you don't have to explain. I just wanted to know.'

'So you are angry.'

'No, I——'

'I'd rather you came straight out with it, Emma. I don't want you harbouring any resentment because I didn't discuss it with you first.'

Which was precisely the point she had had in mind. He had presented this as a *fait accompli*. 'And what else have you to tell me? Have you started looking for somewhere to live?'

This time he blinked several times. 'Well, yes, as a matter of fact, I have. I've actually—well, I've already got it organised. I'm moving into a flat in Ealing this weekend.'

An awkward silence hung in the air as they looked at

each other. It didn't matter now, any of this, yet in spite of that and in spite of herself she was beginning to feel angry with him.

'Look,' he went on uncomfortably. 'It doesn't mean we'll see less of each other, not much anyway. Perhaps just a little less often during the week, but at weekends——'

'No.' The word came quietly but firmly, and she made herself meet his eyes. 'Alan, I'm sorry, very sorry, but our engagement is off.'

It was awful. He was stunned, staring at her as if she had struck him physically. 'You can't be serious! You're not calling off our engagement because I've——'

'No, it isn't because of this, any of it.'

'Then what *is* it, for heaven's sake?' Before she could answer, he started nodding slowly, as if some great realisation had dawned. 'You've met someone else, is that it? Someone in America?'

'No. Well, yes. No, not in the way you mean.'

'Emma . . .'

She closed her eyes, wishing herself elsewhere, anywhere but here, like this. How could she explain what Tor had been to her? She couldn't even explain that to herself, not for the moment anyway. She knew only that she could not get him out of her mind. Even now, throughout this awful, dreadful situation with Alan, she had been thinking about Tor. Even now, she was comparing the two men and, compared to Tor, Alan seemed immature.

Perhaps she had grown up. Maybe, in the six months since she had met Alan last Christmas, when she had been so impressed by things in him which she now saw as unimportant, she herself had had a shifting of priorities.

Yes, that was the case, it was no more complicated than that. She and Alan wanted different things—or at least she was ready, more ready than he, for the things he thought he wanted. Looking at him now, she could not envisage him married with children. He still had wild oats to sow; he would be downright unhappy if he were not out on the town several nights a week.

'I'm waiting, Emma.'

She smiled at the forcefulness in his voice, suddenly realising that his reaction to what she had said was wrong, quite wrong. Oh, he had been shocked at her telling him their engagement was off, but he had not been angry and he had not been *upset*. In that moment, she knew without a shadow of a doubt he was relieved. Relieved! Every bit as much as she was.

Yet, oddly enough, he continued to push her for an explanation. 'What about this person in America? What happened?'

'Nothing.' She smiled inwardly, assuming that Alan's ego was feeling bruised. Well, perhaps it was only fair to give him some explanation. After all, it wasn't every day that he experienced a broken engagement, no matter what his deepest feelings on the matter. 'There was someone to whom I was attracted, but nothing happened.' At his sceptical look she felt a resurgence of anger. 'You can believe me, Alan. You know me better than that. More importantly, this man—well, we talked. We talked about a lot of things, including life and marriage. He had been married and very happily so, so he was a better authority on the——'

The telephone interrupted her. In a way, she was glad

because there was little more she could add, really. She glanced over her shoulder as she headed towards the phone, noting that Alan's expression was still dubious.

'Brownings.' She spoke without thinking, automatically answering the telephone as she would have had she been downstairs in the shop. 'May I help you?'

'I think I can help you,' a voice said. It was a female voice, a self-satisfied female voice. 'With a little information.'

Emma held the receiver away from her ear, looked at it and then shrugged. 'Yes?'

'The reason Alan Dobson didn't meet you at the airport this morning is because he spent last night with an acquaintance of mine. Of the female variety, of course.'

'Of course,' Emma got in quickly. 'But of course!'

'You don't believe me? Then try asking your fiancé about the date he had in Basingstoke, about the flat in Moor Road where——'

'Just a minute! I have a little information *you* might be interested in—I haven't *got* a fiancé.' She hung up at once, furious and disgusted.

'What was that all about, Emma?'

She rounded on him, so angry that her vision was blurred, her hands shaking madly as she struggled to get the diamond ring off her finger. 'That,' she managed, 'was one of those pathetic types who delights in making trouble.'

'What? What do——'

'Moor Road. Basingstoke! Yes, you might well look at me like that.' The ring was off. She marched over to him, holding it aloft. 'Take it!'

'Emma, I can explain this——'

'Don't bother. No, I mean it. I don't *care* what you were doing last night—nor do I care who you were doing it *with*!'

'Just listen a moment! Emma, I only want——'

'I said I don't care.' Nor did she. What she did care about was her own idiocy in trying to explain *herself* to him. Just thinking of all the guilt she had suffered while spending time with Tor, while he, Alan, was . . . but it didn't really bear thinking about.

She took a deep breath and struggled for composure. 'Take the ring back.'

'I don't want it. I want you to keep it.'

'*Take* it!' She almost shouted the words. Almost, but not quite. For the sake of what they had once meant to one another, or at least had thought they had meant to one another, she was trying very hard to retain a little dignity now, for both their sakes. 'Just take it, please, and go. Go, without saying any more, please.'

But that was, it seemed, too much to ask. Though he did have the good grace to blush deeply over what had just happened, Alan did not have the good sense to leave things alone. 'I can't leave it at that. I want——'

She assumed he wanted to explain. She was wrong, but that did not become apparent because she did not let him finish his sentence. 'Well, I neither need nor want an explanation, Alan. You're a liar and a hypocrite—and you had the *gall* to look dubious when I told you I'd remained faithful to you. Heaven alone knows how many women you've been to bed with this past six months!'

'One,' he insisted. 'Only the one, I swear it. And I want to know whether—what was the voice like? I can take it that it was a female voice?'

'Yes.' Emma could do no more than stare at him. 'Oh, yes, it was female, all right. And they don't come much more smug. But you don't suppose for one moment that she gave me her name, do you? Who it was is your problem. Now will you please leave?'

He left, looking very sheepish indeed, not that she felt any satisfaction in seeing him look like that. She didn't feel anything at all, one way or another.

CHAPTER SEVEN

LIFE did not feel good. Emma's work in the shop resumed on the Thursday but there was little pleasure in it. Something seemed to be missing in her life and it had nothing to do with Alan Dobson and their broken engagement. She felt no guilt whatever over Alan, yet nothing seemed right with her world. On Friday she was still struggling to shake off this feeling.

'Emma? Your mum's on the phone.'

'Thanks.' She wiped her hands and walked tiredly from the workroom to the shop, where the telephone was. Madeline and her part-timer, Joyce, were serving in here while Emma worked in the back on a wedding order to be delivered first thing in the morning.

'Just a quickie,' her mother said, 'to ask if you'd like to eat here with us tonight.'

It provoked a smile. She might as well say yes this time. If she did not eat a meal with her parents before the week was out, they would start worrying in earnest. They had been shocked, more so than Alan had, when she had told them her engagement was off, which she had done over the phone. 'Yes, Mum. I'd love to. I'm working on a wedding order right now and you know what that means, so shall we say eight o'clock to be on the safe side?'

'See you then. Back to work. It's probably the best thing for you at the moment.'

Emma put down the receiver with another smile. The best thing for her? Some sort of soothing ointment, was it? There was nothing wrong with her! Well, nothing that made any sense.

'We thought you were wanting to avoid us.' This came from Emma's mother, but not until she had served dinner and the three of them were sitting down.

'We're not your enemies, you know.' Her father beamed at her from his craggy, still-handsome face, leaning over to squeeze her hand.

'I know.' Emma smiled at them both. 'Have you told David what's happened?'

'Haven't you?' Her mother seemed surprised. 'Haven't you spoken to him since you got back?'

'No to both questions.'

'Well, we spoke to him last night but we didn't say anything about you and Alan because we felt we should talk to you about it first. I mean, we haven't been sure whether this was just a lovers' tiff.'

'No, Mum. It's nothing like that, it's—the realisation that I would have been making a mistake. Alan Dobson is not the man for me.'

She watched the exchange of looks between her parents, knowing that her answer, honest as it was, would prevent further questions.

'That's all right, then.' Her father looked at her keenly and, seeming satisfied, nodded. 'We don't expect you to talk about it, love. We understand. Better now than after they'd tied the knot, eh, flower?'

The flower he was addressing was his wife. It was, and had been for as long as Emma could remember, a family joke that Father would never have married Mother had she not been named after his favourite flower, the iris. Another joke was that he had wanted to name his first daughter Rose, but his wife would have none of it.

Whether this were true or not Emma did not know to that day. 'I'll talk to David myself on Sunday,' she said, 'and tell him about me and Alan.'

On Sunday afternoon she did just that. David sounded very chirpy. 'Emma? Hi! Why haven't I heard from you before now?'

'Why haven't I heard from you?' she countered, smiling.

'I knew you were safe. The parents told me they'd picked you up at Heathrow.'

She plunged straight in. 'Well, the latest news about me is that I've broken my engagement to Alan.'

There was a momentary silence, then, 'Can't say I'm altogether surprised, Emma. I always had this feeling he wasn't right for you.'

Emma didn't comment. It was just another example of the knowingness she and David had about one another, although she had denied it, even resented it when David had said words to this effect when she was staying with him. 'So that's that. Now tell me how you are, and how is Anna?'

'Gorgeous! She's due any minute. It's nine-twenty here. I'm feeling better by the day, Sis. Do you think that has anything to do with Anna being in my life?'

'Shouldn't think so. No, nothing at all. Idiot!'

'If there is an idiot in this family, it's you,' he retorted, but there was no longer any humour in his voice. 'When you disappeared for a while last Tuesday morning, I assumed, no, I took it for granted, that you'd slipped next door to say goodbye to Tor.'

Emma's hand tightened around the receiver. 'No, I walked up the road to the local chemist's. Sorry, drugstore.'

'Well, never mind about that. Why on earth didn't you say goodbye to him? He was terribly put out.'

Again her hand tightened. 'Why? What did he say?'

'Nothing.'

'Nothing?' Nothing!

'*You* might be ill-mannered but he isn't. The man has breeding, Emma, he wouldn't be so gross as to point out your shortcomings to me. Not that he needed to. It was downright bloody rude of you to leave without so much as a goodbye!'

The vehemence in her brother's voice startled her. He certainly felt strongly about this; she couldn't recall hearing him swear before. 'But if he said nothing, why are you telling me he was put out?'

'Because he was. I knew it from the look on his face.' Having said that much, David then treated her to a long silence which she tried to ignore, holding back her further questions until she could bear it no longer. She had hardly been able to get Tor Pedersen out of her mind all week; almost every hour of every day she thought about him, but she kept telling herself it was only due to the unsatisfactory conclusion to their relationship.

Whatever the cause, she was desperately curious, now, to hear more about him—and the silence David was giving her was quite deliberate. 'Go on, David. I'm defeated. Tell me more about the look on his face.'

'He was shocked—and that's all I'm going to tell you.'

'Yes, well, I've had enough of your mischief. You're not the same man I used to know and love, David Browning. Quite frankly,' she added, lying in her teeth, 'I'm not terribly interested in Tor and his reactions.'

'Oh, dear. I've gone too far, haven't I? I shouldn't have teased you like that. Of course you're interested. But I don't honestly know what went through his mind when I told him you'd left. He just looked shocked. He said nothing, though—you know he's a man of few words. He is with me, at any rate. With you it was a different story, wasn't it? All that about his wife, I'd known nothing about that. Emma? Are you still there?'

Emma was still there and, to her amazement, she found herself weeping a little, just a little. But she didn't want David to know it. She struggled to sound normal. 'Yes. And yes, it was—he and I were on the same wavelength, I won't deny that. He—let me put it this way: I realised with him what is possible between two people. I seemed to know him so well in such a short time. And it was the same with me. With him, I mean. I'm—what I'm trying to say is that I'll always be grateful to him for that.'

'Are you crying, Emma?'

'Of course not! Why should I be? Listen, this phone-call is costing me a fortune . . .'

'You can afford it.'

'*You* could afford it. Big shot scientist.'

'Hard-boiled young woman. Who do you think you're kidding? Listen, Tor asked me for your address. He said something about writing to you. I'll bet he wants to give you a piece of his mind.'

'Maybe. He'd be entitled. Anyhow, I'm about to ask you for his telephone number. You're quite right about my rudeness, and it's something I intend to put right immediately. In fact, I should have done it before now.'

'I won't argue with that.'

Emma jotted down the number he gave her and said

goodbye. She picked up the receiver again at once to dial Tor—then she put it down again, realising that the prospect of speaking to him was vaguely frightening. Why? It was ridiculous to feel like that. Taking a firm hold on herself, she picked up the receiver and dialled, reminding herself that this was not the first time in her life that she had owed someone an apology.

'Tor? This is Emma . . .'

'Emma?'

'Emma Browning.' He sounded distant, vague, and again her hand was tightening around the receiver.

'And what can I do for you?' He was angry with her, there were no two ways about it. His voice was nothing less than frosty.

'You can allow me to make an apology,' she said, adding hastily, 'I shouldn't have left without saying goodbye, without thanking you.'

Silence.

'Tor?' She spoke when she could stand it no longer.

'Acknowledged,' he said. But he had taken his time about saying it, and he had done so quite deliberately.

At her end, Emma held the receiver at a distance and looked at it as though it had bitten her. Well! She had made her apology, hadn't she? And now what? First, his one-word answer—and now yet another silence. 'OK,' she said crisply, seeing exactly how the land lay. 'Since I've said what I called to say, I shall now say goodbye.'

'Goodbye,' he said, and hung up.

Emma was left with the receiver in her hand, staring at it again. A moment later she burst into tears, and a moment after that she was pacing round her living-room and talking to herself angrily. 'You *fool*! What did you expect?

What, exactly? Why did you bother? He didn't even recognise your *voice*!'

She reached for a tissue and blew her nose. It was minutes before she calmed down, before she could put things into perspective. What *had* she expected? A conversation, at least. Oh, an initial reaction of annoyance, yes, that would have been understandable, but she had not expected to be frozen off the telephone line. And to think she had been all set to tell him about her journey home, about her reaction on seeing Alan, about her breaking her engagement. Oh, yes, she had been quite prepared to do that.

'You're a fool,' she told herself again. 'Tor couldn't care less about you and your life. As far as he's concerned, you are now a million miles away and that's an end to it. He's rich, he's handsome, he's successful, he's extremely self-confident and he's way out of your league. He's also lonely, though he may not realise it, and he's by no means averse to enjoying female company. Because he happens to be choosy, too, and by no means an egotistical man, he doesn't jump in and out of bed with women. He neither wants nor needs that scene. Having said all that,' she added, reaching for another tissue, 'he happened to find you attractive, probably because he saw in you a decent face and figure, possibly because you were unattainable. No, *probably* because you were unattainable.' She finished her mild tirade silently. Unattainable. Forbidden fruit. And, human nature being what it was, that could be very attractive indeed.

At length she went into the kitchen. She had to make herself something to eat. She had to stop thinking about Tor, stop being affected by someone she was never likely to see again. She had, in other words, to get herself and her life back on an even keel.

It was easier said than done. During the following week Emma worked like a demon, grateful that business was brisk. There was, of course, no letter from Tor. Not even a postcard. She had not expected any communication from him . . . nor had she been able to stop thinking about him. She had faced the fact that she missed him terribly, but it was not until he turned up in person that she finally admitted the full extent of her feelings towards him.

It was on a Tuesday morning that he turned up, right there in the shop, just nine days after her phone-call to him. She was in the workroom when Madeline popped her head round the door.

'Emma?'

'Mmm?' She didn't even look up, concentrating on what she was doing, and in that particular instant Tor Pedersen was a long way from her thoughts, which made a change.

'There's someone asking for you, Emma. I mean in the shop. I mean, not on the phone.'

At that, Emma turned to look at her. 'Not on the—what's the matter?' The woman was behaving very oddly, jerking her thumb over her shoulder and glancing heavenwards at the same time. 'One of the bereaved, is it?' She half smiled. It was by no means unheard-of for people who were newly bereaved to come in personally to order flowers—and to start crying when they did so. Madeline never had been comfortable when that happened.

'Bereaved? Hardly! No, it isn't one of those, it's—what can I tell you? A man. A big, blue-eyed blond, built like a Viking!'

Emma's hands started trembling. She looked down at them, at their stained grubbiness, part and parcel of the floristry business, and wiped them against her equally stained overall. Not Tor! Not now. Not when she looked such a wreck.

Not *here*!

'I'm—oh, ye gods!'

'No, I wouldn't go that far,' Madeline said drily. 'He's a bit too mature for an Adonis.'

And Emma was no Aphrodite. 'Madeline, help me! Put him off, I mean entertain him for a few minutes. I must at least wash my hands and face——'

'I'll have you know I'm a happily married woman, otherwise I'd——'

'Madeline! If you value your job——'

'All right, all right. I get the message.' The look in her eyes was something of a revelation to Emma. They had a good relationship but she hadn't realised how fond of her Madeline was. 'I'll tell him you're on the phone upstairs.'

It was amazing what could be done in five minutes. In that short space of time, Emma whipped off her overall, brushed her hair, washed hands and face, applied lipstick and slipped out of the scruffy, flat-heeled old shoes she always wore when she was working at the bench.

At the sudden and unwelcome realisation that it might not in fact be Tor who was waiting downstairs to see her, she started laughing. The laughter had a touch of hysteria in it, however, because she knew very well that it was him.

Mentally and physically she gathered herself together and walked slowly to the stairs, trying to school her features into impassivity. The hurt she had felt at his rudeness, his coldness on the telephone, had fled. In any case, to some extent she had deserved that, or some of it. What mattered now was that he was here, and she intended to make him welcome. A friendly welcome would be in order, but not more than that, just a very pleasant, 'Hello, Tor! How lovely to see you. Do come in. Can I offer you a cup of coffee?'

Then she was face to face with him, under-rehearsed and almost stammering. 'Tor, I wondered . . . so it is you. Er—Madeline, Madeline here, mentioned there was a blond gentleman . . .'

He smiled. It was a calm sort of smile but his pleasure in seeing her showed in his eyes. 'Emma. It's good to see you again.' With that, he took hold of the hand she had proffered, not to shake it but to raise it to his lips.

She blushed to the roots of her hair, which was caused partly by the fact that Madeline managed to catch her eye and grin, but mainly by the impact Tor's presence had on her. His presence and his appearance. His presence, that intangible something which always dominated the space he was in, was not new to her. It was just shocking to experience the power of it again. But his appearance was new, to Emma at least, because she had only ever seen him dressed casually; never before had she seen him looking so strikingly and seemingly bigger than ever in a dark, beautifully tailored suit.

She struggled to recapture the dialogue she had planned. 'It's good to see you, too. Um—can I offer you a cup of tea or something?'

'Thank you.' He turned to Madeline, his smile causing her to blink several times in rapid succession. 'If you'll excuse us, Madeline?'

'Of course.'

The wretched woman did it again. The instant Tor turned his back, she looked straight at Emma and let her eyes roll heavenwards. The look spoke volumes, and Emma had to stifle the urge to laugh. Yet in a way it did her a favour; somehow or other it helped her over a difficult moment and she found herself able quite naturally to turn to Tor as he followed her upstairs, and to tell him laughingly that he had made an impression on Madeline. 'I didn't realise how easy it is for you to turn on the charm, Tor.'

'Why do you sound surprised?' he asked casually. 'I seem to recall that during our last encounter you were convinced I was the most devious seducer of women.'

Emma wasn't having that; he was misquoting her. 'Not convinced, just suspicious. Tea or coffee?'

'Coffee. I'll bet you only have instant.'

'You'll win. Will it do or will you have tea instead?'

'It'll do. This is nice. It's also a surprise.' He was looking round the room, his narrowed eyes telling her he really was surprised.

'Why so?'

'That's a good question. I'm not sure. I'd somehow expected your flat—your flat above your shop—to be . . . makeshift. Yes. Like my apartment in Virginia. Not quite home, as such. But this is a home. There's nothing temporary about it. It's very warm, very cared-for, very . . . let me see . . . cosy. The flowers and plants soften it, of course, but the walls, the carpet, the curtains, the lamps. Beiges, browns, corals. It's soft, Emma.' He turned to look at her, straight into her eyes in that way so familiar to her. 'You are a born homemaker.'

She had perched on the arm of an armchair and she was frowning now. 'I don't know about that. I believe that what's without is a mirror of who's within, if that makes sense.'

'It makes perfect sense. Witness my apartment in the US.'

She glanced away. There was no answer to that. She could not be sure what he was saying about himself. 'I'll put the kettle on,' she said, moving towards the kitchen.

'David tells me you've broken off your engagement to Alan Dobson.'

The words came casually, but they stopped Emma in her tracks. She turned to face him. 'That's right.' Was that why he was here? *Was* it?

He gave her no clue. He said simply, 'Can you come out to lunch with me?'

'Yes.' She didn't hesitate. Why play games? She wanted more than anything to have lunch with him.

It was from the kitchen that she asked the burning question, putting it as lightly and casually as she could. 'How come you're in England? Something to do with business, I suppose? Your writing? Or your father, perhaps?' She heard his low, rumbling laughter, such a familiar sound, and felt a *frisson* of excitement run up her spine. Then she felt scared suddenly. Why hadn't he warned her he was coming? Why hadn't David, for that matter? He must have known Tor was coming to England. He *must* have. 'Tor? I asked——'

'I heard you. I was amused at your mentioning business, my writing and my father all in the same breath. I am here on business, sort of, though I could have dealt with that over the telephone, I suppose. At least at this stage.'

'You're not making much sense.'

'No. I know. That's because I refuse to hold a conversation with you at a distance. I'll tell you why I'm here when you come in.'

When she emerged with the coffee-tray, he did just that. He went straight to the point. 'I'm here to apologise for the way I spoke to you on the phone last week. To be honest, I hadn't got over my anger at your leaving without saying goodbye—goodbye at the very least.'

She nodded, but she didn't believe him. People didn't cross the Atlantic in order to make apologies—and she said as much.

'They might if the circumstances are right. If, for example, they've been missing a person—and if they learn that that person is no longer tied to another person. And,' he added with deliberate mischief, 'if there's unfinished business between the parties concerned.'

Emma looked away, at a loss what to make of him. It was impossible to tell to what extent he meant what he'd just said—and to what extent he was being flippant.

'Your coffee.' She put a cup on a side-table near him and he caught hold of her wrist, startling her.

'What's the matter? Are you still angry with me—about that phone-call?'

'No. I suppose I deserved it. I wasn't angry so much as hurt, anyway.'

'And now?' It was a good question, one she could not begin to answer. Over and above her delight at seeing him, the sheer pleasure of seeing him, she was feeling suspicious. What had the remark about unfinished business been meant to convey? What did he expect of her? The last time she had asked him that question, he had said 'I want nothing of you.' He'd said that he thought they were friends. But she had been engaged to Alan at the time . . . which was no longer the case.

'Emma? A penny for your thoughts now?'

She opened her mouth to answer him flippantly but that was as far as she got, because she heard the sound of her father's voice and then her mother's, and their footsteps coming up the stairs. She glanced quickly at Tor and said, 'My parents. Something must be up, they don't normally drop in when the shop's open.'

There followed ten minutes of conversation which could only be described as babbled, the beginning of which was about Emma's elder sister Janice having gone into labour, the phone-call which had been made by her husband, and Jim and Iris being about to drive down to Devon to help out—and the fact that, while all this had been expected, it shouldn't have happened until next week.

Interspersed in all this was Tor's very warm and enthusiastic 'How marvellous!', a hasty introduction made by Emma, several questioning glances at her, made by her father—and Iris Browning's very obvious enchantment with her daughter's visitor.

'And what about Janice's other two children?' Tor was asking. 'Did they arrive early? And what ages are they?'

'Just a minute!' Emma cut in, laughing. 'Why don't we all sit down and I'll fetch two more cups of coffee.'

By the time she emerged from the kitchen Tor was the topic of the conversation.

'I must say, it's very nice to meet you. We've heard

about you from David, of course.'

'And Emma,' her mother put in. 'She mentioned how kind you'd been in showing her around when she was in Virginia.' That her mother's glance was meaningful when she turned to Emma, only Emma would detect. At least, she hoped Tor would not pick up anything significant in the glance. With him, one could not be sure. But to Emma it said a lot; it asked questions and it communicated understanding of some sort.

Only casually had Emma mentioned Tor to her parents—she had not enthused and she had not mentioned how good-looking he was. What David had told them about him was unclear except that he'd mentioned Tor's being a writer. This was brought into the conversation by Emma's father, who asked outright about the things he had written other than his children's stories.

Tor cited a couple of travel books, one adventure and two spy novels and a series of articles he had written both for English and Norwegian newspapers—none of which Emma had known about.

She said as much, almost accusingly. 'You never told me about any of these!'

He turned to her calmly, his smile nothing short of devastating. 'We had other things to talk about, didn't we, Emma?'

She felt the curious glances of her parents and responded with a warning glance of her own, telling them silently not to ask too many questions. There was only one more, from each of them, both predictable and harmless.

Her father spoke first. 'Have you come to England for a holiday, Tor?'

'It's business and pleasure. I'm here,' he added, while Emma wished he were not adding anything further, 'in Winchester, that is, specifically to see Emma.' In the face of their surprised silence he added, 'Of course Winchester and its surrounds will be well worth seeing, too.'

'Oh, indeed.' Iris Browning glanced at her daughter uncertainly before asking her question. 'So how long are you staying?'

Tor seemed vaguely amused. 'I don't know.' The answer came laconically, and he looked at Emma rather than Iris. Then, to Emma's profound annoyance, he went on, 'How long I stay will depend entirely on your daughter, Iris. I'm about to take her to lunch, then I'll be checking into a hotel.'

'A hotel? But there's no need for that!' At Emma's swift and panic-stricken look, her father held up a hand, smiling. 'No, love, I'm not about to suggest that Tor stays here with you, even if you have got three bedrooms more than you need. I don't think that would be the right thing for a father to suggest,' he added, amusing himself if no one else.

Emma had no idea what was coming but it was time to interject in any case. High time. 'My father,' she said, looking at him pointedly, 'is originally from Yorkshire. That means he's very blunt at times.'

'I see,' Tor said, looking decidedly amused now.

'What we can do,' Jim went on, standing up to extract a ring of keys from his pocket, 'is give you the use of our house.'

Emma said nothing.

Iris said, 'Oh, what a lovely idea! Why didn't I think of it?'

Tor said, 'That's a very kind thought, Jim, but I couldn't do that.'

'Why not? We're not going to be there, remember? We'll be in Devon for at least a couple of weeks, helping in the menagerie. You'd be doing us a favour, house-minding for a bit.'

'You'll find everything neat and tidy,' Iris went on, almost defensively.

It must have been that that persuaded Tor because he looked straight at her and smiled warmly. 'I don't doubt it for one second, Iris. Then thank you. I accept.'

Still Emma said nothing. She could think of nothing to say.

There followed a bit of talk about there being plenty of food in the freezer and where towels and various other items could be found—until Iris pointed out that Emma knew where everything lived.

'Of course,' Jim said. 'Of course she does. Right, then, come on, flower, we must make tracks now.'

CHAPTER EIGHT

'NOW you *are* angry with me. Admit it, Emma.'

'I'm not angry with you. Why should I be?'

'You shouldn't. All I did was accept your parents' very generous offer. It was spontaneous and kind of them and it would have been offensive to refuse.'

'I happen to agree entirely. They took an immediate liking to you.' They were in the garden restaurant in the Royal Hotel and Emma was not, as Tor correctly sensed, entirely at ease.

'Then what's bothering you?'

'Families,' she said with a wave of her hand, 'can be a pain in the neck at times.'

Tor looked surprised, very much so. 'Not yours, surely? I envy you your family, Emma! David, your parents, they're such nice people and——'

'Of course they are!' She spoke airily, waving her hand again, dismissively this time. 'And I love them to bits, naturally. But,' she added, so intensely serious that it brought a smile to his mouth, 'I have had to train them since—well, since I was in my late teens, I suppose.'

The smile turned into a bark of laughter. 'To *train* them? To what, for heaven's sake?'

'To mind their own business in certain matters. Gently but firmly I have communicated to them, all of them, Janice included, that when it comes to me and my private life, they must not try to interfere or to pry.'

'And do they? Try, I mean.'

'They never interfere.'

'Then what's bugging you now?'

'Too many questions. If I hadn't shot warning looks at Mum and Dad, they'd have bombarded you with questions.'

Tor looked highly entertained, entertained but also at something of a loss to understand her. 'Good lord, Emma, I could have handled that! I'd have enjoyed it. What's wrong in someone showing an interest?'

'Nothing, provided that's all it is. I'm very close to my family but—well, family bonds can be oppressive at times.'

'I wouldn't know.'

'Quite. That's why I'm telling you.'

'Then I'll take your word for it. That is, I'll accept that that's how it seems to you. Personally, I could never find having a family oppressive. As for your relationship with David, I think it's wonderful.'

'That is different,' she agreed. 'I'm extremely close to him but even he has boundary lines. Mind you,' she added, smiling and unthinking of what she was saying, 'he has this knowingness about me anyway, just as I have about him.'

'Let me guess—has this got something to do with Alan? I mean that funny little smile on your face. Did David dislike him?'

'No. He only met Alan once—but he did remark to me in Virginia that he was not the man for me.'

'But you already knew that, didn't you?'

'Yes,' she admitted. 'And I was wrong not to face it earlier than I did.'

'We live and learn. Now, I wonder what your sister

Janice will produce? A boy and a girl, like you and David?'

She looked at him gratefully, appreciating his change of subject and the fact that he asked no further questions about Alan. But it was all right, she was more than willing to talk to him about it, if he was interested; she had more than enough trust in him to be able to do that, even if she was suspicious about his motives for being here. In one way, it was as if there had never been any kind of unpleasantness, any disagreement between them. They had been enjoying one another, had been as spontaneous as they had always been—although, of course, that might be a different story once they were alone and in private.

She looked at him directly. 'Aren't you curious about Alan? I mean, about his reaction when I broke off with him?'

'Very.' His gaze was equally direct. 'But I don't want you to talk about it if it hurts.'

She smiled inwardly at that. Did it hurt when he spoke about his wife? Yes was the answer to that. She had seen the pain in his eyes whenever he had mentioned Pamela. But it wasn't the case with her. 'No, it doesn't hurt. I'd been under a lot of illusions with Alan. Or perhaps they were self-delusions, though I'm not sure what the difference is. I suppose I thought I could change him.'

Emma talked openly, and one thing led to another. In no time they were into a discussion about relationships, relationships other than family ones. When the waiter came to offer more coffee they both accepted, and it was at that point that Tor picked up on an earlier remark Emma had made. 'It's surprising, when you come to think about it, how we can meet someone new, like them enormously, or even fall in love, and then immediately begin to try to change things about them.'

He was not, absolutely not, making a point specifically about her. Nevertheless it struck home because she had not herself thought about how common a response this was. In her own experience alone she had been guilty of this several times. There had been boyfriends in her past whom she would have changed, regardless of her liking them very much. She glanced quickly at the man facing her, hoping she would never attempt to do this with Tor. There was nothing about him she *would* change, she felt certain of that. But . . . how long was he going to be around in any case?

He had made it plain that he was here specifically to see her, that the attractions of Winchester were merely a bonus, but she still didn't know why or what it was he expected of her.

'Your business in London,' she probed. 'You said you could have dealt with it over the telephone.'

'That's right.' The blue, blue eyes were steady on her. 'But I chose not to. Since I was coming to see you anyway, that seemed pointless. So when I arrived here yesterday morning I got the business out of the way, straight away, before coming to see you.'

'I'm intrigued,' she smiled, keeping her voice light.

Whether Tor deliberately misunderstood her or whether he truly misunderstood, she couldn't tell. He answered as if it were his business that was intriguing her. 'The BBC want to make a serial of one of my children's books, *The Curse of Murphy's Ring*. I spent all of yesterday discussing it with my English publishers and my agent. My editor here happens also to be an old friend, so we went on to dinner and carried on chatting.'

'And?'

'I'm considering the proposition.' He shrugged. 'We'll see. My agent's very keen, but then he would be, since he wouldn't be involved in the work it would entail.'

And what of his old friend, his editor? Emma asked how he felt on the matter.

'She,' he corrected. 'Her name is Lydia Moss and she's very, very much a she!'

He smiled—while Emma made a conscious effort not to frown. Very, very much a she? And he had dinner with her last night? Perhaps she was more than just an old friend . . .

'If you don't mind,' he was saying, 'I'm a little up to here with this business, Emma. I need to get away from it in order to reach a decision—if you see what I mean.'

'I think so.' She smiled, suggesting that he might like to leave now and take a look at his temporary home.

He surprised her. 'Certainly not. I thought we'd do a bit of sightseeing this afternoon.'

'But, Tor, I can't really abandon my shop . . .' Her voice trailed off. She was looking at him and smiling at the way he was smiling. Of course she could abandon her shop. Why not? Provided she could get Joyce to work full time for a few days, what was the problem?

They used Tor's car, a BMW he had hired, and took a look at Stonehenge before going into Salisbury. The cathedral was first on their agenda, after which they floated in and out of several excellent bookshops. By the time they went back to the car Tor had an armload.

'I can see it now,' Emma teased him. 'You'll spend just

a few days here and you'll know more about my birthplace and its surroundings than I do.'

'But of course! It's the nature of the beast.' He put his books on the back seat and turned to her, laughing as he buckled his seatbelt. He caught hold of her chin, turning her head towards him. 'As for you,' he went on, too seriously for her comfort, 'by the time I leave you, Emma Browning, I shall know all there is to know about you, too.'

Something resembling dismay settled inside her, and it was much to her relief that he turned his attention to driving. So how was she to interpret that? Surely there was only one way it could be interpreted: he was convinced they were going to have an affair. Well, if that was what he supposed, he would have to think again . . .

'Emma? I said I'll need directions to your parents' house. About how long will it take us to get there from here? It would be handy if we could get there before five-thirty, I need to make a couple of calls to London, just to leave messages. I'll have to let my editor and my agent know the telephone numbers where they can reach me.'

Emma glanced at her watch. 'Plenty of time. You'll be able to do that before five-thirty.'

Iris had left everything spick and span, hasty departure or not. As soon as Tor had left his messages in the various offices, Emma showed him the whole of the house, suggesting he slept in the second guest bedroom because it was nearer the bathroom.

'You'll find hangers in the wardrobe,' she told him. She opened the doors of it and turned back to look at him, smiling. 'I mean the closet.'

'I speaka da English.' He laughed, catching hold of her by the waist. 'Now come here, I want you closer.'

'No!' Rapidly she stepped back, hearing and not caring about the anger in the single syllable. She had to protect herself, she had to make a few things clear to him, very clear, and the sooner the better. 'Listen to me, Tor. No, *don't* touch me, please!'

'Hey, what is this? Take it easy, little one, all I want to do is to kiss you! Well, that might not be strictly true but——'

'Stop it. I mean it. Save the soft talk and spare me the charm. I want to make you understand something: I am not going to, I will not, end up in bed with you, if that's what you're supposing. You can *forget it.*'

'Emma! My dear, dear Emma.' He stepped back a pace, leaned an elbow on the windowsill and stared at her. 'What are you afraid of? Why the outburst? What's going on here?'

'Nothing's going on. Nothing's going to go on, that's precisely my point.'

Their eyes locked. Neither of them moved a muscle. It seemed an eternity passed before he responded, 'Do you want me to leave right now, Emma?'

No. Oh, no, that was the last thing she wanted! She was in love with him, she had finally acknowledged that much earlier in the day, when she had first come face to face with him. Looking back further, she could even pinpoint when she had fallen in love with him—though she had been a very long way from acknowledging it at the time, of course.

But she was frightened, afraid of the extent of her own emotions and in a way she was frightened of him, that he might persuade her to do something she didn't want to do, because in the doing of it she would lose him. Whatever they had going for them she wanted to retain. Of course she wanted more, much more, but since that looked highly improbable with Tor she could at least maintain their friendship. 'No, I don't want you to leave, I want us to be friends, but I will not be taken for granted.'

His eyes narrowed. 'Have you met someone else? I mean——'

'I know what you mean. No, of course I haven't.'

He considered this, and her, for a long time. 'All right,' he said at length, still contemplating her closely. 'You have my friendship. That's not new, I gave you that in Virginia. But there's no way I'm going to promise to leave it at that, Emma, because frankly I find it very difficult to keep my hands off you.'

He did keep his hands off her. He kept his physical distance to the point where Emma came very close to making the first move again. It was, she thought, bizarre; she was constantly aware of him, not only in the confines of his car, not only when they were alone in her parents' house or in her flat, but when he wasn't even there. In bed at night she was aware of him. Snatches of conversations would run through her mind, or perhaps just a look on his face, the way he smiled at her; it was like a perpetual and almost unwelcome film going through her mind. Almost unwelcome, but not really. What she really wanted was to be in his arms, to let loose the desire she felt for him, to demonstrate her love . . . but she dared not.

She was for ever reminding herself that he would be gone in a few days. He had mentioned during their lunch at the Royal Hotel that his father was due to arrive in London on Sunday, and that he would be going to spend a few days with him there, in his father's apartment on Park Lane. And after that? She wasn't sure. He might well take off for America or Norway or—who knew where?

Janice gave birth to twin daughters on the Tuesday night. A phone-call was made by a very excited, very proud father to Emma's flat at a quarter to midnight. She and Tor had just got in from a late dinner and he had insisted on seeing her safely inside.

'Congratulations!' Emma turned to Tor, covering the mouthpiece of the receiver to tell him she was now an aunt to twin girls. 'Oh, Michael, that is wonderful! And they're perfect? How's Janice doing? Good. Good . . . My friend? Oh, you mean Tor? Yes, as a matter of fact, he's here now. Sunday? I'd love to come down! I'll talk to you before then, though, to you or to Janice. Right. Yes, same to you, lots of love to you all . . .'

At midnight Tor left, making no attempt to kiss her goodnight in even the most casual way.

The three days after that were wonderful. She became aware of a fundamental shift in her relationship with Tor. They drove and they walked—here, there and everywhere; they laughed a lot, they had serious conversations and a couple of heated discussions about matters to do with the world in general. Not once did Tor make a move towards her, but it wasn't just that that was different, nor was the shift in their relationship a bad thing. On the contrary, Tor was more attentive than ever, seeking to please her as much as she sought to please him. *That* was what was different—he was more considerate, more sensitive towards her than ever, and sometimes during a silence she would turn to him and catch him watching her, a thoughtful expression on his face.

On the Friday afternoon she had no choice but to work. She explained to Tor that she had to help Madeline with the orders to be delivered on Saturday.

'Fine,' he said happily. 'Find me a stool in your workroom and I'll watch you. I'd love to do that. You wouldn't mind, would you?'

'Not at all. But—are you sure? You could be doing other things. Won't you be bored?'

'I'll soon find out.'

He wasn't bored, he was fascinated; he even ended up putting two simple bouquets together and he did it remarkably well, choosing the variety of flowers himself and working within the costing she gave him. He was only defeated by the wiring of the bow around the Cellophane. He even offered to help with some deliveries on the Saturday morning, insisting he knew the area well enough by now, but Emma drew the line at that, although the gesture pleased her.

'Absolutely not, but thanks for the offer. No, tomorrow I shall work from eight till around twelve and then we'll have lunch and decide what to do with the afternoon. Madeline and Joyce can cope without me in the afternoon.'

'How about driving to London and doing something there?'

They went to Madame Tussaud's and the Planetarium, from which they emerged into pouring rain and tried in vain to find a taxi to take them to where the car was parked.

'It seems a bit silly, really,' Emma said, 'your driving

me back to Winchester now when you have to be back in London tomorrow morning. I could take the train back.'

'The train?' Tor looked at her blankly, as if she'd said something in a foreign language. 'What do you mean, I have to be back in London tomorrow?'

'Your father. You told me he was arriving at Heathrow in the morning——'

'Oh, *that*. Didn't I tell you? I spoke to him late last night, from your parents' house. He has to stay in Norway. Some hitch over something or other. He's had to postpone his time in London.'

'Oh.'

'Oh.' He smiled at her, his arm encircling her shoulder as they finally found a free taxi. 'So I'm coming with you to see Janice and the new babies tomorrow—unless you, or anyone else, feels I shouldn't . . .'

'No problem! You're more than welcome, Tor.'

It was still raining when they got back to Winchester. 'Are you hungry?' she asked as they approached the city. She was thinking ahead.

'So-so.'

'Same here. How about fish and chips tonight?'

'A wonderful idea! I love English fish and chips. Shall we eat them at your place or mine?' He grinned, turning his attention from the road. 'Or shall we sit in the car and eat them, fresh from their wrappings?'

'Certainly not! There's a super chip shop just a few doors away from my shop. So turn left here and go straight on at the lights—provided they're showing green, of course.'

'Oh, *Emma*! That old joke. Must you?'

When they got indoors, she left Tor to his own devices

and went downstairs to make an arrangement of flowers—but first she telephoned her sister to explain that she would not be alone on her visit the next day.

Janice was home and was delighted at the prospect of her visit with Tor. 'There's only one problem—we can't put you up for the night. What with *four* children and Mum and Dad——'

'We wouldn't expect it, Jan, we'll leave early in the morning and we'll take off from you after tea; we'll have dinner on the way back here.'

Twenty minutes later, at the sound of Tor's voice, she jumped, turning to look at him with wide eyes. 'Gosh, you startled me. I've been quite carried away here.'

He came up behind her to look over her shoulder, his hands resting lightly on her upper arms. 'That is exquisite, Emma! Just beautiful. You're so artistic. Those tiny flowers, isn't that commonly known as baby's breath? And the crib, the way you've arranged all those tiny pink rosebuds, it's delightful.'

'It's appropriate.' She shrugged, feeling acutely aware of his touch, casual and light though it was. 'Would you go for the fish and chips now? I'll get my hands clean then I'll butter some bread for us. Cod for me, please; they'll cook it while you wait.'

Tor had been gone less than five minutes when a call came for him. It was his editor. 'I'm sorry to disturb you,' the voice said to Emma. 'My name is Lydia Moss and I've been trying to contact Tor Pedersen all afternoon. Is he there, please?'

So this was Lydia Moss, editor and old friend—the one who was 'very, very much a she'. Well, she certainly had a very feminine, velvety voice, a really distinctive voice.

'He is, but he's just popped out,' Emma said politely. 'He might be fifteen, twenty minutes or so. Shall I ask him to call you back? Has he got your home number?'

'Thank you. He has, but I'm going out in ten minutes. Still, there's no particular hurry, if you'll just ask him to ring me when it's convenient for him——'

'Certainly.'

By the time Tor came back it was too late for him to return the call. He shrugged it off anyway, muttering something incoherent about it. Emma had set the table but he insisted on eating his fish and chips from his lap, fresh from their wrappings, as he put it. She laughed and let him get on with it.

Ten o'clock found them sitting on her three-seater settee, together but apart, in the midst of a gripping film showing on TV for the first time. When it finished they discussed it briefly, thrashing out their differences of opinion on one particular point. Tor laughed at her, teasing her about her vehemence, reminding her that what she had just seen was only a film and not reality.

'But it *could* have happened, Tor. If——' That was as far as she got. She was drawn into his arms and, while she might have had time to escape the embrace, in truth she didn't want to. All week she had been longing for this, she had been longing for it and at the same time defended against it. The attraction between them was so powerful, so much that even as his mouth came down on hers now she was telling herself that a solitary kiss would be all they would exchange.

Indeed it was, except that the kiss went on and on, ever deepening and increasingly sensual as one moment melted into the next.

When at length Emma drew away from him she was cursing herself; they were both breathless and the look on Tor's face told its own story. She should have called a halt sooner, considerably sooner. Desire for her was stamped all over his features. But he said nothing. He merely looked at her, uncomprehending.

'I'm—would you like a drink, Tor? I mean a drink-drink.'

'No. I'm going now.'

She blinked in surprise, it was so abrupt. 'But—why? What's wrong? Would you prefer a cup of tea, given that you've to drive——'

'I don't want a drink of any kind.'

He was already on his feet and she got up, too. 'Tor . . .'

'I'll tell you what's wrong. You. Me. This.' There was plenty of warning this time, she saw what was coming but she made no attempt to sidestep him. Nor did she move into his arms. She merely stood still when he embraced her, neither encouraging nor discouraging—until he bent his head to kiss her again.

'No. That's not a good idea, Tor.'

'Isn't it?' he said coldly, drawing her impossibly close, holding her so tightly against the length of his body that she was aware of every inch of him. Then he was kissing her with a force which at one and the same time excited and repelled her, bruising her mouth with the sheer hunger of his own.

He eased up only slightly, but at just the right moment his tongue moving shockingly, deeply into the warmth of her mouth. A groan which seemed to come from her soul tried and failed to escape from Emma, resulting in an erotic little sound that Tor reacted to by raising his head, by holding her at arm's length and shaking her.

'Now tell me to keep my hands off you! Go on, tell me this isn't what you want. Look at you, you're trembling. So say it, lie to me again if you will!'

It was true, she was trembling, but she was also angry, with him as much as with herself. 'I've no intention of lying to you, I simply don't want to go to bed with you.'

'Why? Why not?'

She stepped away from him, well away. 'It's just the way I feel, I——'

'That doesn't make sense.'

'Perhaps it doesn't—to you. But you don't care about my feelings, do you?' Angrily she added, 'You're too concerned with your own. Well, that's not good enough, and I will not allow you to trample over *my* sensibilities.'

'Emma——'

'No! I mean what I'm saying, Tor, whether it makes sense to you or not. So go, will you?' Defiantly she lifted her chin, deliberately looking him in the eyes as she added, 'Since we're not going to end up in bed together, you might as well.'

He held the look, and in those few seconds Emma realised several things. He would leave, he had recognised the challenge implicit in her last sentence—and it had angered him. The quietness in the way he answered her confirmed that. 'I will go, but I'm not going because I might as well, I'm going because I want you so damn much that leaving you is the only sane thing I can do right now.'

In three strides he was across the room, and the door to the stairs was open. 'Don't forget we have an early start tomorrow,' he flung over his shoulder. 'And I hope you sleep well, Emma . . .'

'No, don't come to the door, Janice, stay where you are and keep your feet up.' Janice's husband, Michael, spoke very firmly to her even if he did manage to blow her a kiss in mid-sentence. 'I'll see Emma and Tor out.'

'I'll see them out.' Emma's father got up, as did her mother, and in the end everyone was at the front door, including Janice's four-year-old daughter and six-year-old son.

It had been a full day and it wasn't over yet. Tor drove in silence for a long time and Emma was glad of it. She had been aware of her distraction, her quietness all afternoon, but there had been so much going on in her sister's house that nobody else had noticed it.

'You've been quiet all day, Emma.'

She laughed in spite of herself. How typical it was of him! She might have known. Did he miss nothing? 'How could I compete against that cacophony?'

He grinned and that was all it took to make her heart twist painfully. There was a flash of pure pleasure on his face, which was just an added problem for her. She had seen that look often today. Tor's enjoyment of her family, most particularly of the children, had touched her deeply at some very tender level she hadn't known was in her, not to such an extent. He was a born family man, through and through. Oh, he had so much love to give, if he did but know it!

Alas, he didn't know it, not any more at least. Whether it was there in such abundance because he had been deprived as a child of a family's warmth was immaterial. For whatever reason, it was in him. But Tor had brought down the barriers against that kind of loving when his pregnant wife had died. He even believed himself past it or beyond it or no longer interested, or something.

She wanted to shout out in frustration.

As if it would help, she closed her eyes and breathed deeply, but once again unwanted pictures flashed against her closed eyelids: Tor being handed the two newly born babies by Janice, the look on his face, the wonder, the tenderness in his eyes . . .

Janice had seen it instantly, so had Iris, and they had both turned to glance at Emma—but when Michael had made some joking remark about Tor's handling of the baby girls he had shrugged it off and said something about beginner's luck.

'Emma?'

'What did you say? Sorry, I was nodding off.'

'If you say so. I was asking whether you're hungry. Would you like to stop soon? We're about half-way back to Winchester.'

Already? Maybe she had nodded off. 'Well, I'm not in the least hungry but I'm happy to stop if you are.'

'Just for gas then. I'm stuffed. Your mother makes a mean afternoon tea, so-called.'

'It wasn't the tea, it was the lunch she produced. She's always been like that. I don't know how her children all managed to grow up slim.'

'It has to be the eighth wonder of the world.' Which would have been fine, left as a joke, but Tor put his hand on her thigh and caressed it very provocatively, very deliberately. 'I must say that Mrs Browning's youngest daughter has the most delectable of shapes . . .'

Emma gave him no feedback, thinking it was better to

say nothing at all. She simply lifted his hand from her thigh and put it back on the steering-wheel, ignoring his soft laughter.

When they finally got to her flat and Tor had parked at the back of it, she yawned and told him not to bother seeing her inside.

He didn't even credit that with an answer, but got out of the car, opened the passenger door, put a hand under her elbow and firmly helped her to her feet. She took one look at the inscrutable expression on his face and knew that a protest would be a waste of breath.

'How do you think I manage,' she said haughtily as they climbed the stairs, 'to get in and out of here at night when you're not here?'

'I dread to think. It's spooky out there and you'd have no chance if—but you're a gutsy girl, aren't you, Emma?'

'Am I? I've never thought about that. I'll put the——'

'Don't say it, let me guess. You're going to put the kettle on, right? Don't you English people ever do anything else?'

'Ha! So says the Norwegian Englishman who lives in America and loves their coffee.'

'I don't live in America. I spend only half my time there.'

'And the rest? Exactly where? Oslo? You have an apartment there, haven't you?'

'No, I sold that when Pam died. I have a house now, not in Oslo, in Bergen, on the west coast.'

When he followed her into the kitchen and draped an arm around her shoulder, Emma stiffened slightly in anticipation, and, Tor being Tor, he felt her response immediately.

'You can take it easy,' he said, smiling without humour, his blue eyes fixed firmly on hers. 'It's been a long day and I had very little sleep last night . . .'

He left the sentence hanging in the air, and Emma looked away. She hadn't slept very well herself the previous night.

'So don't make tea for me,' he went on. 'I'm going now.'

'Tor——' She spoke his name as he reached the door and he turned, looking hopeful, making her wish she had let him go without another word. 'I—just wanted to thank you for today,' she said awkwardly. 'It was a long drive and——'

He smiled; again it was without humour but it was, at least, a gentle smile. 'I should thank you,' he said softly. 'I enjoyed being with your family. I enjoyed it very much indeed.'

She stood motionless as he left, staring at the door he had closed behind him. Whenever he left her, it was as if the sun had gone out, it was as if a big chunk of her own vitality left with him. She sighed, acknowledging how very much she loved him—and wanted him. Tonight she was feeling it acutely. That look on his face just now, when she'd called him back and he had looked at her hopefully. Oh, how very easy it would have been to open her arms to him, to beckon him silently into them!

Resisting her own desire, resisting him, was by no means easy. Virtually all day, for six consecutive days, they had been together—and the tension was mounting . . .

Miserably she turned to pour boiling water into the teapot, hating the dilemma she was in. Tor had said nothing about leaving Winchester, not yet, but it was of course only a matter of time before he took off. And if she did go to bed with him? Would he come back?

And if she didn't?

CHAPTER NINE

AFTER a very early start in order to do her buying, Emma had to work in the shop the following morning. Madeline had a dentist appointment and Joyce, her part-timer, telephoned at eight-thirty to explain that she couldn't come in.

'I can't oblige today, Emma. I'm sorry, but——' But her little girl had a high temperature and Joyce was keeping her from school. She had sent for the doctor. 'It's probably something and nothing. At least, I hope it's nothing serious.'

'I hope so, too, Joyce. Do ring me and tell me what the doctor says.'

So that was that. Emma hung up and immediately rang Tor. He answered on the first ring. 'Tor, hello—it's me.'

'Good morning, little one. I was just about to ring you, in fact I was just reaching for the phone.'

'Then I'd call this good timing. Listen, I can't come out to play today.' She laughed, going on to explain about Joyce and her child. 'And Madeline has an appointment at the dentist. All being well, she'll be in at lunchtime, but I thought I'd put you off this morning. I don't want you to be bored, hanging around waiting for me.'

'I'm afraid I can't come at all today, Emma. I'll see you for dinner, of course, and we'll go somewhere different. Somewhere in Salisbury, perhaps.'

She was not put out by this, but she was surprised. 'Has something happened?'

'No. Lydia wants to see me, that's all. Hence her

phone-call the other day. I'm meeting her at the office for an early lunch, but, knowing how it is when we start talking shop, it'll go on into the afternoon. So I'll pick you up at . . .' He paused to think. 'I'd better say seven-thirty, Emma. All right?'

'Fine. I'll look forward to it. Shall I book somewhere in Salisbury?'

'Better not, just in case I'm a bit late. There's probably no need on a Monday anyway, we'll go on spec.'

When eight o'clock rolled around and there was no sign of Tor that evening, Emma recalled their conversation, thinking that it would be a bit silly to drive over to Salisbury at this time. Even if he arrived within the next few minutes, it would mean they would be eating very late.

By eight-thirty she was beginning to worry.

He arrived at eight thirty-five, apologising profusely. 'Roadworks on the motorway. No sign of them this morning—you know how it is. I was in one of those situations; I didn't know whether to stop at the motorway services and call you, but I thought it a waste of time—better to drive on and get here. You know how it is.'

She smiled, reaching to smooth the frown from his forehead. 'You've said that twice. Yes, I know how it is. So you've driven straight from London? It must have been some meeting—you look tense.'

'I'm fine, Emma. My main concern was being late for you. What Lydia neglected to mention was that Harry Black was joining us after lunch. He turned up at her office at three.'

'Am I supposed to know who Harry Black is?' she

teased, sensing the tension in him in spite of his denial. She had never seen him like this before; he was edgy, seeming ill at ease.

'Sorry. My agent. I could use a drink, Emma, have we got time?'

'We have all the time in the world, we're not going anywhere.'

'What do you mean——?'

'I mean,' she said firmly, 'that you're going to sit down and relax. Have a drink or two, or even three. You can always take a mini-cab back to my parents' house.' She paused, expecting him to suggest, jokingly or otherwise, that he could equally stay the night with her.

No such comment was forthcoming. Rather he wanted to know what they would do for food.

'I have a deep freeze, I have a microwave.' She shrugged, uncaring that the evening was not going to be as planned.

'That sounds like a lot of hassle, and in any case I keep my promises. Just give me ten minutes and we'll go out to eat locally.'

'No.'

He smiled finally, easing himself into an armchair and looking at her. 'No, Emma? That's something you're too fond of saying to me. You could be making a big mistake . . .'

She kept her face straight. 'By cooking dinner for you?'

'By continually saying no. Wretched woman!'

'Oh, well. Never mind. We all make mistakes, don't we?'

Tor laughed at her flippancy, her apparent

nonchalance. 'Come here, you.'

She went to him. His arms were open and there was
something, just something about his mood tonight, his
attitude, that conveyed to her a certain vulnerability. It
was out of character and it was something she couldn't
help but respond to. There was something on his mind,
something to do with this business in London, and she
hoped that by the time the evening was over he would tell
her about it. For the moment—well, for the moment he
seemed in need of a good, old-fashioned, plain and simple
cuddle.

He gathered her into his arms and pulled her on to his
lap, nuzzling his face against her hair. 'Mmm . . . you
smell good, my darling. And you look good . . .'

She had taken pains with her appearance, her make-up,
her hair. It was loose, the way he liked it, and she was
wearing a flowery, summery dress with thin
shoulder-straps and a full skirt, the kind that swayed about
her legs as she walked.

For several minutes they held one another, without
kissing, without talking, both content just to be in close
contact. 'Food,' she said at length, brushing her lips
against his brow as she made to move away. And he let
her go, too, which surprised her, although she didn't show
it.

By the time they had finished the meal she had put
together it was turned ten o'clock and Tor had had several
drinks—two generous measures of scotch and the best
part of the wine Emma had opened to have with their
dinner. She had done most of the talking, and he had said
very little. This was not unusual, for he was more than
capable of stretches of silence—but tonight it was
different. Tonight their silent times were not shared, not

comfortable. She could still sense that he was troubled. He didn't follow her into the kitchen as he normally did, when she was making coffee after stacking the dishwasher, and it was during those few minutes alone that she decided to prompt him into talking.

Deliberately she sat next to him, close to him, on the settee. 'What is it, Tor? What's on your mind? Perhaps I can help, if only by listening . . .' Her voice trailed off because he had turned to look at her with an odd expression on his face, as if her words had not made sense to him. 'Tor?'

What happened next was the last thing she expected. He drew in a sharp breath, speaking her name repeatedly as he pulled her almost roughly into his arms. 'Emma . . . Emma . . . have you really no idea . . ?' Then his mouth was on hers, and she was locked against him in a vice-like embrace.

Inwardly she panicked, but she made no attempt to fight him off because she knew with utter certainty that to do so would be pointless. This passion, this fervour in him, was something over and above anything she had experienced before. It was and it was not . . . *right*, somehow. All her instincts screamed this information at her, though she could not really make sense of it. It was as if he were being driven by something else, something beyond a physical need. But what? *What*?

'Tor——' Beneath the onslaught of his mouth it was impossible to say more, so it was when his lips moved to burn a flaming trail along her neck to her throat that she spoke his name. Again and again she spoke his name, feeling an unprecedented need to communicate with him, really communicate. 'Tor, Tor, what is it? What *is* it?'

'You. It's you, Emma.' She heard the words, she tried to assimilate them, tried to interpret what they really meant—but she failed. She failed because the shoulder-straps of her dress were pushed aside and the swell of her breasts were exposed—all of which happened in one smooth, easy movement. Everything changed again. Her brain began to slow down. Her body began to take over. When his lips moved to her breasts, her thinking became fragmented, layered somehow. On one level she knew that what was happening was not right, not only because she didn't want this but mostly because Tor's urgency had some deeper motivation behind it.

But on the simpler, physical level, she was responding in spite of herself. The feel of his lips against her breast, first the full, firm flesh of it and then against the most sensitive part, already taut and hungry for his caress, was almost more than she could tolerate.

And yet again she experienced a dual response. She wanted to push him away and she wanted this sensation never to end. She wanted more. But something, somehow, was *wrong*. 'Tor, please . . . please!' With a tremendous effort she pushed him away, just enough so they were no longer in such intimate contact.

'Emma, for heaven's sake——' His voice, thick with desire, was barely more than a whisper.

As he reached for her she moved back sharply, pulling the straps of her dress into place. 'No, *don't*. This is all wrong, Tor, and I want——'

'*Wrong*?' He cut in on her raggedly, staring as if he had never seen her before. 'Wrong, Emma? What's that supposed to mean? I'm well aware that you don't take sex lightly, but you're not turning puritanical on me, are you? I can't believe this!'

'I didn't mean that, I meant it feels wrong because——'

'It feels very right to me.' Again he interrupted her, reaching out to gather her into his arms. 'Let's go to bed, Emma. Now.'

'No.' The word came icily, deliberately so, and she drew away from him easily this time; he made no attempt to stop her.

'Why? Tell me why.'

'Because I don't want to.' There was still frost in her voice.

'Now that isn't true, darling.' Tor managed a smile but, to her extreme irritation, he spoke to her as if she were ten years old. 'That simply isn't true. Come on, tell me about it.'

In sheer frustration she got to her feet, needing to put distance between them. 'That's precisely what I want you to do, Tor. Tell me about it, tell me what's bothering you. You're different tonight, and I want to know what's wrong.'

He looked bemused, as if he were unsure whether she was serious. 'There's nothing different tonight. I—the situation,' he added more firmly, pointedly, 'is the same as every other night. I want you. I want to make love to you and I know damn well you want this, too. I've been getting contradictory signals from you for days. I've respected the fact that you must have your reasons for hesitating, though heaven alone knows what they are.'

Emma looked steadily at him, realising she was getting nowhere. But she wasn't mistaken, she was almost certain of that. He *was* different tonight. 'So you're not going to tell me what's on your mind?'

His laughter annoyed her further. 'I just have. Emma, you're free, you're no longer engaged, you have nothing to feel guilty about any more, so what gives?'

'This won't work,' she said coldly. 'You won't talk me into bed. It's been tried before.'

Again he laughed. 'I don't doubt that for one moment. You're being obtuse, Emma. Why are you making things complicated? Why are you making such an issue——'

'I'm *not*! I—look, just leave, will you? If you're not prepared to talk to me, go home.'

He got to his feet, frowning, and placed his hands firmly but gently against her cheeks. 'That won't do, not this time. We won't resolve this with anger.'

It looked to Emma as if they wouldn't resolve it at all.

Tor persisted, going on to tell her it was she who was different tonight, not he. 'Tell me what you're afraid of, Emma, then we can sort it out. Tell me. It's that simple.'

That simple? Oh, if only he knew! Of course it would be simple for her to make a fool of herself and tell him she loved him. It would be simple to accuse him of being interested only in her body—but that would be a dishonest accusation. In other words, there was nothing remotely simple about it. 'I'm not afraid of anything. I just don't want to have an affair with you.'

To that he merely shook his head, making it very plain that he didn't believe her. 'My dear Emma, from the beginning you were never disinclined, only guilt-ridden because of Alan. But that's all finished with, so why don't we——'

'Let go of me!' she snapped. 'And leave Alan out of this. It has nothing to do with him, or with guilt, or with fear.' She stepped away from him, glaring at him. 'I'll tell you this much: I'm tired of this ongoing argument, and I'm tired of your persistence. It isn't amusing, it's offensive. Do you understand me? You have no respect for the way *I* feel.'

'I have every respect for the way you feel.' His response was angry, too—telling, as it always was, in the very quietness of his voice. 'But I have *no* respect for your lies.'

'*Lies*?' Her own voice came loudly, indignantly. They were getting nowhere, they could go on like this for hours—which she was not prepared to do. 'Get out of here, Tor! I'm very tired and I'm in no mood for this.' With that she turned her back on him, evoking a response that shook her.

'All right, I'll go. Dammit, Emma, I've never met anyone as stubborn as you. I'm going, and I'm not coming back. Perhaps that'll satisfy you—it will certainly put an end to our arguing!'

Dazed, she sank into a chair when he'd gone. Not coming back? Surely he didn't mean that? Surely it had been said in the heat of the moment?

There were no tears. She was too stunned for tears. Over and over she told herself that Tor couldn't have meant it. It couldn't happen, not . . . just like that.

In the early morning she heard the sound of a car outside the front of her shop. She heard something being put through the letter-box and she knew it was not the postman who was delivering. It was too early for the postman. When the car drove away she got out of bed and pulled a cotton housecoat around her.

On the floor behind the door was a letter and a bunch

of keys on a ring. They were the keys to her parents'
house. In the letter was a cheque made out to her father.
The letter said, 'Emma, this cheque is to cover the
telephone calls I made from your parents'—many of
which were overseas calls. I'm moving back to London
this morning. I'll be at my father's flat.' There followed
the telephone number there, with, 'Ring me when you
feel so inclined, when you have calmed down and you're
ready to talk, really talk. Failing that, I see no point in our
continuing, Tor.'

Calmly Emma took the keys and the letter upstairs to
the flat, knowing already that she would telephone Tor.
There was no way she was going to finish this on such a
sour note. That had happened once before, but it wasn't
going to happen again. What the outcome of her call to
him would be she had no way of knowing yet. Nor did
she know when she would ring. Not today, probably. Let
him calm down, too . . .

She pottered into the kitchen, almost smiling at her last
thought. What it really meant was: let's see if he rings me
first.

He didn't ring her. All day, as one long hour followed
another, she waited for Tor to ring her. Business was brisk
but it did not stop her from thinking about him every
minute, no matter what she was doing. Her emotions
fluctuated wildly, from distress to anger to fear. What if
it was over between them? What if it really was over?

On Wednesday, when she could bear it no longer, she
rang him at lunchtime. There was no answer. She rang
again at seven. Still there was no answer. At that point she
decided to take herself out for the evening. Tor was
probably out for the evening. She would try the number

again later.

It was quite late when she got home. She had registered hardly anything of the film she had been to see—and the new restaurant she had then gone into had produced a very poor meal. She wasn't feeling any better, either, for having given herself a change of scenery. Wherever she went, Tor was there. In her mind and in her heart he was there. The question was, could they resolve their differences? Or, rather, *how* could they? She wanted more than an affair, much more, but he ... Perhaps it would be for the best if they did finish. A future with Tor was not merely highly improbable, as once she had thought, it was probably impossible. He was no longer interested in commitment of any sort, not since Pamela.

Having made herself a cup of coffee she then sat, looking at the telephone as if the instrument itself might suddenly produce a solution. She couldn't produce one, her mind behaving like a carousel going round and round and getting nowhere. Finally she picked up the receiver, knowing by then that there was nothing for it but to play this conversation by ear.

There was no conversation. This time the telephone was answered—but not by Tor. Emma recognised the voice instantly, there was no mistaking it. Lydia Moss answered with the number in her velvet-smooth, very distinctive voice. It was then that Emma glanced at her watch and, on seeing it was ten minutes to midnight, it was then that she understood.

Somehow she managed not to drop the receiver, she managed not even to slam it down. Wordlessly she replaced it with a strange, almost frozen calmness. Lydia Moss! So she *was* more than just an old friend. Lydia

Moss, in the apartment with Tor, at this time of night . . .

And what of Monday, when Tor had spent the day with Lydia?

With sickening clarity everything fell into place. Emma knew, now, what had been wrong about Tor when he had turned up late on Monday evening. He had spent the entire day with Lydia and they had *not* been talking shop all day. Emma had not actually thought about this before but, focused on it now, she recalled that Tor had been just about to leave for London at eight-thirty on Monday morning. Why? That was far too soon to leave even for an early luncheon appointment. And how did she, Emma, know he had been telling the truth in saying that his agent had joined them in the afternoon? How did she know he was late getting back to Winchester because of roadworks on the motorway?

What did she know, actually?

One thing. If nothing else, she knew that Tor Pedersen was a two-timing bastard!

Not content with Lydia, he wanted her, too. Why? Because having two women on the go suited his male ego? Because the relationship with his 'old friend' was waning and Emma was going to be the replacement?

She felt sick, mentally and physically, and it was a very long time before she managed to get some sleep that night.

CHAPTER TEN

IT RAINED heavily on Thursday. It suited Emma's mood. Madeline was in the shop with her but there wasn't much to do, so it didn't matter that Joyce was still off, looking after her little girl. The child had developed measles.

Late in the afternoon a young man of about eighteen came in and asked Emma for a dozen red roses. Shyly, feeling self-conscious if not a little silly, he checked with her that in the language of flowers twelve red roses meant 'I love you'.

She had to put him right. 'I'm doing myself out of some profit,' she said laughingly, feeling touched and sympathetic, 'but no. Twelve means, "Let's be friends". If you want to tell someone you love them, you send *one* red rose.'

He looked dubious, asking her anxiously whether she was sure of this. 'It's what I was taught,' she said. 'By my father, and I very much doubt that he had it wrong.'

'Then give me one, please. But put it in a box or something, would you? I don't want her to think I'm mean . . .'

No sooner had he left than the telephone rang. Madeline answered it and wordlessly waved the receiver at Emma. Madeline had recognised Tor's voice, and the look on her face was all the warning Emma needed.

She braced herself. 'Emma Browning speaking.'

'Emma? It's me. What's the matter? You sound uptight.'

Something far stronger than anger flashed through her. 'Uptight? Yes, you could say that. But *I* have nothing to say. I have nothing whatsoever to say to you, Tor. Not now, and not ever.'

She hung up at once and excused herself to Madeline. 'I'm going upstairs for a bit.'

It would soon be closing time; she was thankful for that. Even before she had reached the top of the stairs, the telephone was ringing again. She ignored it, knowing it would be Tor again and knowing that Madeline would cope. Madeline would think of something to say.

Ten minutes later it rang again—and that was enough to tip the emotional scales for Emma. She burst into tears.

She was still crying when Madeline called up to her, very tentatively, 'Emma? I'm about to lock up, OK?'

'OK. I—was that him again?'

'No. The first call was, the second was business.'

'What did you tell him?' Emma appeared at the top of the stairs and looked down, dabbing at her eyes and not caring what she looked like.

'What could I say? I don't know what's going on, but—well, I suppose you've had a row.'

'More than that. It's over, Madeline.'

'Oh! I—I'm very sorry to hear it, I really am. I thought you two were . . . well, never mind. I just told him you weren't available, Emma. What else could I say?'

'Nothing. You said the right thing. Thanks. Goodnight, I'll see you in the morning.'

She had to get out. There was no way she could stand her own company tonight. But where could she go? To a girlfriend? No. She didn't want to talk about Tor to anyone. To her parents? No. They would know instantly something was wrong, very wrong.

She opted for the cinema again, in Salisbury this time, but it was the same story. Nothing could distract her from thinking about Tor . . . and nothing could stop the anger which continued to boil inside her.

When she drew her car to a halt at the back of her shop, she thought nothing about the one that was parked in the spot next to hers. There were always cars around there, not always the same ones. Only when she opened her door, which brought the interior light on, did she see that someone was sitting in the adjacent car—and that it was Tor.

In no time he was standing outside the vehicle, his eyes looking incredibly beautiful in the lamplight. 'Emma——'

'I told you, I have nothing to say to you.' She marched straight past him to her door.

'I want to talk to you.'

'I just told you——'

'Then listen. Just listen to what I have to say, *then* decide.'

He was standing right behind her, but she did not turn to face him, nor did she put her key in her lock. She simply grasped it in her trembling hand because there was no way she would risk his following her inside. 'Get away from me, Tor. Get back to London and Lydia!'

'*Lydia*? What the hell——' He broke off. There was a two-second silence and then he started laughing. 'I see.'

Incredulous, Emma spun round and saw at once that the laughter was genuine, there was nothing clever or defensive about it. 'You think this is funny, do you? You think it's *laughable*?' Incensed, she raised her right hand, but the slap she so dearly wanted to land on him was deflected.

Tor sobered instantly, gripping her upraised arm so tightly that she feared he would break it. With his free hand he plucked the keys from her fingers. 'Just as well you didn't make contact, Emma. Where did you learn that little trick?'

As if she had thought about that! Doing damage to his face had not been her intent; she had wanted, needed, only to stop his laughter. Now, suddenly, she felt impotent. Tor had found the key to her door and it was already turning in the lock.

'Inside,' he said firmly. 'There's no way I'm going to stand out here talking to you.'

'And there's no way,' she said, equally firmly, 'that you're coming in, either.'

This time she had every intention of standing her ground, implacable though his expression was. What she could not have anticipated was the ground being removed from beneath her. In one second and with one horrified gasp, Emma found herself picked up and flung over Tor's shoulder.

Being carried up the stairs like that was like a living nightmare. Only when they were half-way towards the living-room did she realise it would be in her own interests to stop flailing her arms and kicking her legs. When he flung her unceremoniously on to the settee, she felt very disorientated and, far worse, extremely humiliated. 'How *dare* you? How——'

'Shut *up*, Emma!'

She shut up. Shock prevented her from going on. She had never, ever, heard him shout before—except for that time she had almost crashed into his car. And not only had he shouted at her, he was going on to roar at her now. 'So you called me at my father's flat at midnight last night, and because Lydia Moss answered the phone you put two and two together and made five. Right?'

Emma was staring at him, bemused by the very volume of his voice—and at the same time wondering what fantastic story he was going to produce by way of an explanation.

'Right?' he bellowed, effectively snapping her into action.

'Go to hell!' She was on her feet in a flash—and in a flash she found herself pushed back on to the settee.

Tor stood over her with his big hands clamped firmly on her shoulders. 'Keep still and listen, woman.' His voice had changed. The volume had dropped and the anger had gone out of it, but it had been replaced by an exaggerated patience which made it plain that his anger was still very close to the surface. 'Lydia answered the telephone last night because, I suppose, she happened to be sitting closest to it. She and my father had been out to dinner together.'

Emma could do no more than stare up at him. 'Your f-father?'

'My father. He and Lydia went out alone—and as soon as they came back to the apartment, I went to bed.'

'Your father and Lydia . . .'

'Have had a thing going for many years, an arrangement that suits them both. Emma, Lydia is a very lovely lady, but she's old enough to be my mother.'

'I'm—but I thought——'

'I know what you thought.' He let go of her and she

flopped back against the settee, not knowing whether to laugh or to cry. She felt idiotic. There was no question of whether or not to believe him, she just knew he was telling the truth.

'When did your father come to England?'

'Yesterday. You remember he was due on Sunday? Well, I had to do a bit of running around for him on Monday morning—which I did because it was important to him—business—and because we both thought he wasn't going to make it to England this week. Anyhow, he got his business abroad sorted out and he turned up at the apartment out of the blue yesterday afternoon. He was as surprised to see me there as I was to see him. The first thing he did was to make a date with Lydia, which he always does when he's in London, and I declined to go out with them because I knew they'd prefer to be alone. Also,' he added pointedly, 'I was waiting and hoping to hear from you.'

He moved away from her finally, to sit in an armchair opposite her. 'It wasn't until this afternoon that Dad remembered to tell me someone had called—and hung up—late last night. I put two and two together, and *I* made four.'

Emma couldn't help but respond to that, and to the smile he gave her. When he went on to call her an idiot, she nodded.

'I——' She hesitated then decided to say it. 'I've called you every name under the sun. I thought you were a two-timing bastard.'

He looked heavenwards. 'I wonder if I'll ever understand you fully? I keep thinking I do, but . . .'

They sat in silence for a moment, looking at one

another, until wordlessly Tor got up and helped himself to a drink. 'What will you have, Emma?'

She decided to have a brandy, feeling she could use one. Inwardly her spirits were soaring, she was full of hope and yet, at the same time, she was hardly daring to hope. 'You—began by saying you wanted to talk to me,' she said at length, when they were sipping their drinks and the silence had continued.

'I do,' he said. 'And I'll get straight to the point now. I want you quite desperately, Emma, not that that's news to you. But I can't offer you more than an affair, and my friendship. Having said that, I see no reason at all why we shouldn't enjoy those things. If——'

'Tor, listen——'

'No, just a minute. Let me finish. I want to go on seeing you but as I've told you before, it can't be on the basis of friendship only. That's just not on. I can't handle that, not with you.'

Emma had heard enough. Her heart felt as if it were being squeezed excruciatingly. Beyond a certain respect for his honesty, his laying it on the line, as it were, she also felt a resurgence of anger towards him. Maybe it was unreasonable—and maybe not. She didn't know, perhaps she would never know, because all she had to go on was her feelings, not her reasoning. She loved him to distraction—and he was offering her an affair. Somehow, she managed not to thrash out at him, to shout out the protest coming from her heart. 'The answer is no, Tor.'

He shook his head, impatience creeping back. 'Let me finish, please. Just listen. Now, I've decided to go ahead with this BBC thing. When it starts to happen, I'll be spending a lot of time in England. I'll be around during

the making of it for consultation and advice, which will
be written into the contract. This will all happen in the not
too distant future, by the way. The series is being made
on location in England, in and around London and also
the New Forest. Quite apart from that, I mean the fact that
I'll be around, think of the fun we could have! Europe is
on our doorstep. Paris, Rome, Madrid—there are so many
wonderful places we could visit together, spend long
weekends in if you didn't want to be away from your
business too long.'

Emma looked away, afraid to let him see the emotions
she was feeling. Her business was her last consideration.
Her first consideration was her *self*. Oh, yes, certainly he
was painting a pretty picture and she knew he would be
as good as his word, that together they could have
marvellous times. Of that she was in no doubt. But it
couldn't be. Did he have no idea how she really felt about
him? Had he not begun to guess? Perhaps she should tell
him? No. Not that.

And he hadn't finished yet. 'Emma, I'm not just
offering you a few days of rolling in the hay, I know that's
not your style. It's not the nature of the beast.' He broke
off, smiling, looking at her while she looked away again,
feeling wretched.

It took an effort to make herself meet his eyes again.
'Offering?' she said quietly. 'What exactly are you
offering me, Tor?'

He looked confused, as if he was convinced she had
failed to understand him—or that she hadn't been
listening. 'As I've said, an ongoing relationship which
might last . . . who knows? Years.'

Emma took another sip at her drink. All her anger had

dissipated because Tor had at least meant what he'd just said. He was, at least, sincere. But it was a prospect she would not even consider. It was not without allure, not compared to the prospect of never seeing him again, but it was not on, either. An ongoing relationship? Yes, she wanted that. But she wanted a whole lot more besides.

But how was she going to tell him this?

How was she going to answer him?

An ongoing relationship. Oh, it didn't take much imagination to envisage how it would be for the most part, when she was working and he wasn't, when she was in Winchester and he decided to go back to Virginia to write another book. Or to Bergen or Oslo or somewhere. No. No matter how he presented the idea, he was talking simply about an affair. Quite apart from anything else, he wasn't even talking about togetherness. 'Is that it, Tor?'

'That's about it.' He was smiling again. He drained his glass and looked at her expectantly. 'Well? You've listened, now what do you say?'

Had she not been so very deeply involved emotionally, she might have told him to go to hell. She might have ranted and raved. She might have accepted, even. But involved she was, and right now it felt as if her heart was breaking. 'The answer is no.' She managed the simple sentence, but only just, without her voice trembling. 'And I'd like you to leave now. And this time please stay away.'

He didn't seem to believe her. He stared at her for what felt like an eternity until, once again, she looked away. 'But, Emma, why? It just doesn't make sense. I know you want me——'

It was too much. She couldn't look at him but she could, at least, be honest with him. It was time to tell him.

She would tell him, and then he would go. 'It's rather more serious than that, Tor. I want you, yes, but . . . I happen to love you, too. Very, very much.'

The ensuing silence was one she thought she would not live through. It went on and on. Although she still wasn't looking at him, she could feel his eyes on her. In reality the silence could not have lasted more than a minute. It just felt like a lifetime.

Then, mercifully, Tor was on his feet and reaching for the jacket he had discarded earlier. 'I see,' he said finally, his voice devoid of emotion. 'Then perhaps you're right, Emma. Perhaps I should go away and stay away.'

CHAPTER ELEVEN

TEN days later the memory of that final scene with Tor was every bit as fresh in Emma's mind as it had been half an hour after he had left, after she had embarrassed him into that long and dreadful silence.

Madeline was late, she was normally at the shop by eight-thirty on a Saturday but there was no sign of her so far. It was going to be a busy Saturday, too, because Joyce was unable to come in. Having nursed her daughter back to health, she herself was unwell now.

Emma was in the workroom, sorting out the deliveries which had to be made. She could never not enjoy her work but these days it was by no means as important to her as it used to be. Nothing seemed to matter as much as it had before . . . before Tor. He was constantly in her mind. He was the most important thing to her, regardless of his no longer being in her life. His absence did not change the fact that she loved him. How could it? Loving was not something one could do or not do, feel or not feel, to order.

She was just thinking of ringing to check that Madeline had left home when Madeline rang her.

'Emma? Look, I'm sorry but I can't come in today. I'm feeling rotten. I've just——'

'Don't worry about it. I thought you looked off-colour yesterday, you were feeling rotten then but you kept denying it. I hope you're in bed?'

'Too right. I think it's flu.'

'Let's hope it's just a cold. Anyway, get well soon.' What Emma would not tell her was that Joyce couldn't come in, either.

'But, Emma, it's Saturday—will you and Joyce be able to cope?'

'Of course we can cope. You just concentrate on getting better.'

As soon as they'd hung up, Emma telephoned her father. He and Iris had come back from Devon only two days earlier and, while she was reluctant to ask this favour just now, she could see no alternative. 'Dad? Help! Madeline and Joyce are ill, I've got deliveries to make and it's Saturday.'

'I'll be right there. I'll bring Mum to help you in the shop.'

'To help you in the shop. I'll do the deliveries, I've got a load on, and I know what you'd rather be doing—taking money.'

'Right! See you soon.'

She hung up with a sigh of gratitude, appreciating how good her parents were.

It was around two-thirty before she rejoined them in the shop. It was proving to be one of those days; already they had sold out of roses in spite of their being in so many people's gardens at the moment. Around four o'clock there was an abrupt cessation of customers, and Emma and her parents trooped into the workroom to have a cup of tea. By five o'clock they were busy again and looking forward to putting the 'Closed' sign on the door at six. Saturday was the one night Emma closed at six, as on other days it was five-thirty.

It was five minutes to six when she told Jim and Iris to

call it a day. 'A few more minutes and that's it. Thanks for tidying up, Mum. Thanks for everything, both of you.'

'What are you doing for dinner? Or have you got a date tonight?' Iris looked at her optimistically.

'No, no date.' Emma met her eyes as she answered. It was no secret to any of her family that she was in love with Tor, but nobody talked about it because they knew she wanted it that way.

'Well, why not eat with us?' her father asked.

'It'll be makeshift.' Her mother smiled, unconcerned about showing her tiredness. 'After this little lot today, it'll be something out of the freezer, that's all, but you're more than welcome, darling.'

'Thanks, Mum, but no. I'm going to take a hot bath and after that I think I'll throw something on to a plate and just relax by myself and watch the——'

'Somehow,' her father cut in, 'I don't think you will, Emma.'

There was something in his voice that brought both women's eyes straight to him. He was looking towards the shop door, and Emma followed that look. Just as she registered what her father had already seen through the glass, the door opened and the bell jangled and she felt the blood draining from her face.

She felt her mother's hand touch her shoulder, and heard her mother's cheerful and very natural, 'Tor! What a nice surprise. How are you?'

Emma's ears were ringing. It wasn't fair. This shouldn't be happening. Not again. It was like a punishment. But why? What had she ever done to him that he should haunt her so? There was no calmness in her now; she felt icy cold inside.

If she had acknowledged her appreciation of her parents earlier, it was nothing to what she felt for them in the ensuing minutes. Regardless of their knowing that their daughter had been hurting over Tor, they did not judge. They were friendly and warm and natural towards him, behaving as if they knew nothing. Iris, typically, asked him upstairs for a cup of tea.

The Viking took one long and thoughtful look at Emma before turning to address her parents. 'It looks to me as if Emma could use a brandy. And I think, if you'll forgive me for saying so, that it would really be better if you left us alone. I have to talk to Emma urgently about something very important.'

Emma looked from one face to the next. When her eyes met with those of her father, she saw a dangerous flash in them and she panicked inwardly. Jim had perceived that one of his progeny was feeling threatened, and he was about to defend his child.

Iris, on the other hand, had a deeper understanding of the situation. She spoke up immediately, before her husband had decided what tack to take. 'I think you're right, Tor, she could use a brandy. There are a lot of summer colds going around just now—I hope you're not sickening for one, Emma. Jim . . .'

There was only one second of tension before Jim smiled. 'We were just going anyway. I'll put the sign on the door, Emma, if you want to go upstairs. Will you lock the door after us, Tor?'

If there was a further exchange between Tor and her parents, Emma didn't know about it. She went straight upstairs and poured herself a stiff brandy which she drank in two gulps. She felt the effect of it immediately. There was no effect of intoxication, not even remotely, but it did manage to warm her and help her relax infinitesimally.

Then, inevitably, Tor was in the room with her, standing in the doorway and looking at her. Just looking, wordlessly.

'You look as if you could use a drink yourself.' She spoke with a trembling voice. She was on an emotional overload and could not have disguised it even if she had wanted to, which she didn't. Why bother? He had in any case seen by now that he had the power to reduce her to this state, so why attempt to deny it?

'Thank you. Yes, I could.'

'Please help yourself.' She gestured towards the cupboard where the bottles were kept and held out her empty glass. 'I'll have another. And, Tor, just do me one favour, would you? Tell me why you're here.'

'I'm here to ask you to marry me,' he said.

Emma's glass dropped from her hand.

He picked it up and took hold of her by the shoulders. 'Sit down. Sit and please listen, and please try not to interrupt me.'

Interrupt him? She could do nothing other than stare at him. She watched as he poured drinks into two more glasses, one of which he put on a side-table near her. Emma left it there and waited.

Tor didn't sit down, he seemed unable to keep still. He was not the self-composed, self-assured man she knew; the tension inside him was showing in many ways, in the set of his shoulders, in the way his hand shook slightly when he held his glass to his lips.

'Emma, the last time I walked out of this room, and out of your life, or so I thought, I hated myself. Please believe

that. I had made a proposition to you that sounded shabby
even to my own ears. Shabby, because even then I knew
it wouldn't do, it wasn't the truth. I knew as I talked to
you that I was acting against my instincts—but I was
scared. I was scared to commit myself to more. I even
knew, or at least suspected, that what I was suggesting for
us was offending you, maybe even hurting you. And then
you told me you loved me.'

He paused, sighing deeply. 'I knew you meant what
you'd said—yet I tried to deny it to myself. I tried to tell
myself you didn't really love me, that you're young and
you were probably merely besotted. I reminded myself
that you'd thought you loved Alan, but you'd been
mistaken. In other words, I did everything I could to
convince myself that your love for me was not real, not
the right kind of love.' His eyes moved over her shoulder,
away from her steady gaze, to fix on nothing for a
moment. Then he glanced down at the glass in his hand.
'I'm—probably not making much sense. You may well
wonder why I put myself through these mental
gymnastics, this denial——'

'No,' she interrupted softly. 'I don't. I know why.'

His eyes came back to hers swiftly, holding a mixture
of hope and disbelief. 'How can you?'

She smiled a humourless smile. 'Because I know you.
Because I understand you. I always have.'

'Do you know I love you?'

'Yes, but I didn't always. I thought . . . that you would
never acknowledge it.'

There was pain in his eyes. 'I fought it. Emma, I'm
sorry but I . . .'

'It's all right.' More than anything in the world, she

wanted to get up and move over to him, to hold him in her arms and make him know how very much she did understand about him. But at that instant it would have been the wrong thing to do. It was not the right moment. He needed to talk and she let him, encouraging him to because she knew that the pain she saw in his eyes was about her, her and him. It had little to do with Pamela. Little, but not quite nothing, to do with Pam. 'Say it,' she urged gently. 'You were afraid to love again.'

'To love again. Oh, yes. Lord, yes! Love, commitment, marriage, I was afraid of it all, afraid to open myself to any possibility, however remote, of loving and losing again. At the time Pam died I vowed never to marry again, never again to love. I believed I was safe in any case, because I really thought I could never feel such love for a woman ever again. You see, it happened with you in a similar way it had happened with Pamela. I told you I married her within three weeks of meeting her. Well, with you it was love at first sight, looking back. I told myself at the time, of course, that the notion was ridiculous. I rejected even the concept because I knew it couldn't happen, falling in love like that—a second loving like that could *not* happen twice in one lifetime.'

When he broke off she waited, and when it appeared that he wasn't going to say any more she prompted him. 'Go on, Tor. Wasn't there an element of guilt in all this, as well?'

He smiled, ruefully and with admiration. 'Yes. That came a bit later. That's why I suggested an affair when I knew damn well you wanted more than that. *I* wanted more than that. But somehow I felt I shouldn't, couldn't marry again. I thought a great deal about the mind-sets we take on board—do you remember that conversation we had in Virginia?'

'About the way we often follow the patterns our parents set? Yes, of course I remember.'

'Well, it wasn't the case this time. It was a feeling of guilt towards Pam, pure and simple. Oh, I knew it was illogical—but I felt as if I were being unfaithful to her memory.' Again he paused, looking at her anxiously. 'You're not saying much, my darling.'

'That's because I understand fully what you're saying. It all had little to do with logic.'

'It had nothing to do with it.' At last he smiled, his relief at her response showing clearly in the way his body relaxed. Finally he sat down. 'It was exclusively emotional. It was safer to keep barriers around me.'

He looked at her uncertainly for a moment, until she smiled further encouragement. Her façade was calm now, she knew, but inwardly her heart was beating a frantic tattoo against her ribs. Oh, how she loved him! And thank heaven she had not gone along with that suggestion of an 'ongoing relationship', as he had put it! Had she not stood firm, in spite of the pain it caused her, he might never have realised fully all the insight he had now reached. What a gamble it had been! She shuddered to think about it now, because there had been the very real possibility that he would never have realised any of it anyway, that she would never have seen him again.

'What is it, Tor? Say it, darling, you must see by now that there's nothing you can't tell me. Trust me, and tell me the rest.'

He nodded, returning her smile. Had she not known he loved her, had he not already told her so, she would have learned about it in that moment. His eyes were saying it all; beautiful though they always were, there was an added light in them now, a tenderness she had never seen before.

'The rest of it?' he said. 'There isn't much more. Yesterday was the anniversary of Pam's death. Three years. I was in Paris, I've been spending some time with my old grandfather, maternal. He lives there—but not for much longer, probably. He's eighty-three and in bad health. Anyway, I went out for a walk, alone, yesterday. I was going down a busy street and I must have looked as sane as any other man, one minute. But the next minute I stopped in my tracks and I found myself talking to myself, loudly. I asked myself what the hell I thought I was doing. Pamela had been dead for three years, for heaven's sake, so what did I think I was doing? I was in a place I didn't want to be, without the person I wanted by my side.'

He laughed suddenly, at himself, and shook his head. 'Emma, I shouted out for the whole of Paris to hear, "I want to marry Emma Browning!" And some wit who was passing by spoke to me in English. He said, "Then get on with it, man!" A sensible sort of guy, wouldn't you say?'

'Very!' He had opened his arms and she moved over to him, snuggling on to his lap and nuzzling her face against his neck. 'I'm proud of you,' she said softly.

It was several seconds before he reacted to that, and when he did she could hear the emotion in his voice. '*You're* proud of *me*? That's rich, it really is! Because I can't begin to describe how proud I am of you. I love you, Emma, I love you body, mind and soul.'

'Oh, Tor . . .' She abandoned the rest of the sentence; there was a painful catch in her throat, and in any case she knew another way of telling him she felt exactly the same. A kiss could say it better.

When at last they came up for air, he asked her if she would marry him. To that she couldn't help but laugh. 'You mean you have *doubts*?'

'No, I just want to hear you say it.'

She said it.

'When?' he persisted. 'Will you marry me as quickly as possible? I want you with me always, day in, day out, year in, year out. How quickly can a wedding be organised in England?'

'Well, there could be a problem . . .'

'There could?' He looked shattered, uncomprehending.

'Actually, darling—it's just that I've always wanted a white wedding. But I suppose it doesn't really matter.'

'Is *that* all?' Tor's brow cleared and he leaned back against the settee heavily with relief. 'You shall have precisely what you want. That isn't a problem at all; I like the idea.' He pulled her closer against him, his eyes gentle on hers. 'In fact I love the idea of seeing you walk down the aisle towards me, looking beautiful as you will in some wonderful white creation.'

Emma wasn't comfortable with this, she couldn't be sure he wasn't saying this just to please her. 'Tor, it doesn't have to be like that——'

'Wait a minute.' He held her a little away from him, the better to see her face. 'It's what you want and it's what you're going to have.'

She smiled, nodding. 'I would like a white wedding. I love the idea of walking down the aisle towards you looking . . .'

'Beautiful,' he prompted, smiling at the way she was parroting him.

'Looking *nervous* in some wonderful white creation.'

Tor laughed. 'So be it, my darling! I shall spend the rest of my life doing all I can to make you happy, to please you.'

Once again they were kissing and, again, it was some time before they talked. 'What about our lives?' Emma stilled the hands roaming across her breasts. It was very difficult to think when he did that. 'I mean, where will we live?'

'Where do you want to live? What do you feel about your business?'

'Not a lot, not any more.'

'Then we could live most of our time in England, not far from here. I'd be more than content with that. And in the winters we'll go skiing in Norway. In the summers we can spend time in Paris, if you'd like that. Spring would be the time for New York, of course——'

'Just a minute!' Emma was laughing uproariously. 'How many homes are we going to have? And where is that kind of money coming from?'

'As many as we like, wherever and whenever we like. I'm a writer, remember? One can write anywhere. Have typewriter, will travel. As for the money,' he said, breaking off to kiss the tip of her nose, 'well, let's just say that won't be a problem. What concerns me, my darling, is whether you might feel bored without your work.'

'*Bored*? With all that you've just described? You have to be kidding! Oh, I can't wait to scour New York! I've always wanted to, but all I saw in June was the inside of an airport. Now let me see . . . can we honeymoon in New

York?'

'I don't see why not. I mean, it won't make any difference, will it? It won't matter.'

'What do you mean, it won't matter?'

'Where we are won't matter.' There was a wicked gleam in his eyes when he grabbed hold of her tightly. 'I mean, you won't be setting foot outside the bridal suite anyway—so where we are will make no difference.'

'Mr Pedersen! What *do* you think I am? Some sort of sex machine?'

'I've no idea—yet. I look forward to finding out.' He leered at her, reaching for her again, sending her into a giggling fit with the lecherous look on his face. 'Come closer, little one, and let me start to find out right now what I'm letting myself in for.'

'Tor——'

'I don't believe it!' The telephone had started ringing and their heads swivelled to stare at the instrument as if it were a snake poised to strike. 'I suppose you'd better answer the thing.'

She did. She didn't need three guesses as to who it would be, either, but just wasn't sure of the gender. Her parents. Her mother or her father?

It was Father, a father who spoke so casually that it was laughable. 'Oh, hello, Emma. Just thought I'd give you a quick ring to see if——'

'You can relax, Dad.' She smiled into the receiver, loving him to bits. 'I'm fine. And so is my future husband.'

'Oh, well, that's all I wanted—your *what*?'

'Sssh! Don't say anything! Put Mum on the line, I want to tell her myself.'

'Emma?' Iris's voice was anxious. 'What is it, darling? Is there some awful scene going on there—or has Tor left? Are you——'

'Fine, Mum. Glowing, you might say. But I'm afraid you've got your work cut out for you. Do you think you can organise a nice white wedding very quickly?'

Behind her Tor was laughing, wagging a finger when she turned to smile at him. 'Naughty!' he said when she'd finally hung up. 'Teasing them like that.'

'They loved every minute of it.' Emma flopped down next to him on the settee. 'And I have a message for you, from my father.'

'Fire away.'

'Well, when he came back on the line, he asked me to tell you that he looks forward to having a celebratory drink with you when you get in.'

Her husband-to-be looked blank. 'In? In where?'

'There, of course!' Emma was laughing her head off. 'And the rest of his message was that he's going upstairs now, to make up the spare bed in the guest-room . . .'

HARLEQUIN
Romance®

Coming Next Month

#3103 TO TAME A COWBOY Katherine Arthur
Jennifer needed to get away from the city, her parents' bickering and a violent boyfriend. A ranch in Montana seems far enough, her new boss Clay Cooper a warm generous man. Jennifer begins to relax until she finds herself an unwilling participant in another family's row!

#3104 CITY GIRL, COUNTRY GIRL Amanda Clark
Stung by a bee, knocked down by a huge muddy dog—that's Hannah's introduction to country life. So the last thing she expects is to actually *enjoy* the enforced vacation. Or to fall in love with a country vet named Jake McCabe....

#3105 THE GIRL WITH GREEN EYES Betty Neels
When Lucy meets eminent pediatrician William Thurloe, she determines to become the woman of his dreams. The fact she is neither clever nor sophisticated like Fiona Seymour, who wants William, too, is just one small obstacle she has to overcome.

#3106 OF RASCALS AND RAINBOWS Marcella Thompson
Kristy Cunningham races to Mount Ida, Arkansas, to find her missing grandfather. She runs up against her granddad's young partner and self-proclaimed protector—and the strangest feeling that she must stay, no matter what....

#3107 THE GOLDEN THIEF Kate Walker
Leigh Benedict seems to think every young aspiring actress is a pushover for the casting couch, and his cynical attitude appalls Jassy. But the attraction that flows between them makes it difficult for her to convince him otherwise.

#3108 THAI SILK Anne Weale
Clary helps a fellow Briton in trouble in Thailand by summoning Alistair Lincoln halfway around the world to bail out his stepsister. But when he insists on Clary sharing responsiblity for young Nina, it's Alistair who becomes the problem.

Available in February wherever paperback books are sold, or through Harlequin Reader Service:

In the U.S.
901 Fuhrmann Blvd.
P.O. Box 1397
Buffalo, N.Y. 14240-1397

In Canada
P.O. Box 603
Fort Erie, Ontario
L2A 5X3

HARLEQUIN
American Romance®

RELIVE THE MEMORIES....

From New York's immigrant experience to San Francisco's Great Quake of '06. From the western front of World War I to the Roaring Twenties. From the indomitable spirit of the thirties to the home front of the Fabulous Forties to the baby-boom fifties...A CENTURY OF AMERICAN ROMANCE takes you on a nostalgic journey.

From the turn of the century to the dawn of the year 2000, you'll revel in the romance of a time gone by and sneak a peek at romance in an exciting future.

Watch for all the CENTURY OF AMERICAN ROMANCE titles coming to you one per month over the next four months in Harlequin American Romance.

Don't miss a day of A CENTURY OF AMERICAN ROMANCE.

A CENTURY OF
AMERICAN ROMANCE
1960s

The women...the men...the passions...the memories...

Coming soon
to an easy chair near you.

FIRST CLASS is Harlequin's armchair travel plan for the incurably romantic. You'll visit a different dreamy destination every month from January through December without ever packing a bag. No jet lag, no expensive air fares and *no* lost luggage. Just First Class Harlequin Romance reading, featuring exotic settings from Tasmania to Thailand, from Egypt to Australia, and more.

FIRST CLASS romantic excursions guaranteed! Start your world tour in January. Look for the special **FIRST CLASS** destination on selected Harlequin Romance titles—there's a new one every month.

NEXT DESTINATION:
THAILAND

 Harlequin Books

JTR2

Harlequin Superromance

**Here are the longer, more involving stories you
have been waiting for... Superromance.**

Modern, believable novels of love, full of the complex
joys and heartaches of real people.

Intriguing conflicts based on today's constantly
changing life-styles.

Four new titles every month.
Available wherever paperbacks are sold.

SUPER-1
